THE
Basil Book

THE
Basil Book

MARILYN HAMPSTEAD

Illustrations by Isadore Seltzer
Basil Drawings by Maggie LaNoue

LONG SHADOW BOOKS
PUBLISHED BY POCKET BOOKS NEW YORK

Another *Original* publication of LONG SHADOW BOOKS

A Long Shadow Book published by
POCKET BOOKS, a division of Simon & Schuster, Inc.
1230 Avenue of the Americas, New York, N.Y. 10020

ISBN: 0-671-50685-4

First Long Shadow Books printing August, 1984

10 9 8 7 6 5 4 3 2 1

LONG SHADOW BOOKS and colophon are trademarks of Simon & Schuster, Inc.

Design by Jacques Chazaud

Printed in the U.S.A.

Acknowledgments

There is no doubt a story behind every book ever written. This is a book that almost did not get written. Writing itself is hard enough when you are not a professional writer. Couple that with running a small, highly specialized farm and trying to computerize that farm simultaneously—that's pure madness. Our rental computer ate data discs daily. Our fancy, high-priced, semi-customized hard disc system that followed suffered numerous hardware and software catastrophes, and still fails to fulfill its promise. Yet I yearned for the promise that computerization portends.

Meanwhile, as our mail-order records became scrambled more thoroughly than eggs, tornado winds threatened to devastate our greenhouses, key staff left and other perils endangered this Pauline, my dear family, close friends and staff banded together when I decided to abandon this book in April '84.

Such support cannot go unrecognized. So although *The Basil Book* has my name on the cover, it really reflects the spirit of enthusiasm, cooperation, support and the combined wisdom of the following folks: Donald and Charlie Hampstead, Matthew Zapalski, Leota and Robert Cogan, Janet Isham, Linda Stelle, Kevin Hill, Ron Godden, Kevin Hammond and Mary Konopka.

Support and encouragement frequently come unexpectedly: Jan Longone, at the Wine and Food Library, Ann Arbor, Michigan; Dan and Audrey Buozas, Portfolio Ltd., Pasadena, California; Randall Heatley, Jackson, Michigan and Lorraine Butchart of the Jackson District Library.

And there are significant others whose writings influence this brief tome: M. Grieve, V. Tiedjens, J. Childs, G. Greene, H. Darrah, Monsieurs Funk and Wagnalls, R. Stout, R. Stout, J. Beard, R. B. Fuller, T. Jefferson, Henny Penny and Chicken Little.

And finally a special thanks to Maggie LaNoue of Albion, Michigan, who at the last minute was recruited to do the drawings for the Basil Personality Profiles. She's captured the spirit and the likeness of them, one and all.

Marilyn Hampstead
Fox Hill Farm
Parma, Michigan
May 1984

~ Contents ~

1

Basil:

A Love Story

Basil and I first met one sunny afternoon long ago. I was young and impressionable. Basil's magnetism was highly charged, etheric.

Our first encounter was in my friend Silvana La Rocca's back yard in suburban Detroit. Silvana's father was there working, and we went out to chat with him. The air was hot, heavy and sultry. Already giddy with the natural passions of adolescence, I was overwhelmed by mysterious fragrances and swooned as Silvana's father greeted me with some basil and a handful of some strange-looking tomatoes.

I rushed into the basement kitchen to find refuge with Nona, Silvana's grandmother, who spoke only Italian. She listened sympathetically as I babbled away in Polish about basil. (In my neighborhood on the west side of Detroit, you always spoke Polish to non-English-speaking older people.)

Basil was apparently an effective *lingua franca,* for somehow we were able to communicate. She sat me on a high stool, grinning warmly and nodding. She too knew basil's sensual power. She listened and destemmed. She turned and stirred a pot. Then, like a flash, she took her long, sharp knife to basil. Chop, chop, chop . . . to but a shred of its former robustness. I watched, nervously twirling a naked basil stem, my legs becoming more tightly entwined around the legs of the stool.

Nona buried the basil in a mortar and ground it to a fine paste with some garlic and salt. Next she embalmed the paste in a fruity olive oil and annointed it with parmesan. Turning again to the pot, she quickly snatched out some pasta. To my utter amazement, she poured the basil onto the pasta and gave it to me.

Somewhat startled by green-glazed spaghetti, I reluctantly, but politely, (we were brought up to be always polite to our elders, to do as we were told and to eat what what was served to us) took the plate and cautiously took a little taste. And then I ate it all, asking for seconds and thirds. (Me, with a reputation back home as a finicky eater who would sit for hours at the dinner table staring at big, fat, canned peas!)

My passions were stirred through my tastebuds. It was my coming of age, there in that basement, with sausage that looked like kielbasa but did not smell like kielbasa and those strange tomatoes, small, oblong and flat.

I cherish the memory of my first basil affair, and many years later, I found myself courted by a charming young man who cooked me steel-gray squid with red, beady eyes, tempted me with luscious tropical fruits and bade me to sip Bordeaux until finally, one day, we shared our first conjugal pesto.

That most unlikely triangle—basil, Donald and I—has been a continually strengthening bond, and the force that led to the founding of Fox Hill Farm.

And now the basil beds in Parma hold almost twenty basil brothers from all over the world. I still feel a heightened excitement, a soaring of emotions, as I clamber among them, safe and snug in their beds, each new morn. A soft caress releases their fragrant promise. I pretend to be a mature adult but cannot resist daydreaming, and sometimes I frolic through time and relive history among the leaves of my basil.

And for all that, I give thanks to my mentor Nero Wolfe, to James Beard who let me know it's certainly ok to play with my food, the adventures of M.F.K. Fisher and to Ruth Stout for communicating the nature of growth; but most of all to my dear Donald, my mate.

The Detroit News, *May 20, 1981*
Parma's Fox Hill Farm:
A Heaven for Herb Lovers

"Basil, camphor," says the mail order catalogue form from Marilyn Hampstead's Fox Hill Farm.

Basil, compact bush.
Basil, dark opal.
Basil, fine leaf.
Basil, lettuce leaf.
Basil, sweet.

As exciting as those herbs' names sound to anyone who's ever spiced a sauce or spruced up a soup with the stuff, there's still the niggling curiosity about the smells and tastes you just can't have with a mail order experience. . . .

It's nearly a two hour drive from Detroit, . . . but once you're there that initial curiosity is more than satisfied: you're likely to learn more about herbs from an hour there than any catalogue or book could ever teach. . . .

To those who think of herbs as a frightenly complex and exotic world of mysterious flavors and smells, it's significant to learn that Marilyn Hampstead is self-taught. . . .

"My real start in the awareness of herbs began with my Polish grandmother. . . . Grandmother grew some herbs out in the back yard," she says, "for both medicinal and culinary purposes —horseradish, chives, marjoram, parsley. . . . My primary interest has always been in culinary herbs . . . basically because I love what they do to ordinary dishes."

. . . It's a family-run operation: besides Marilyn and her husband Donald, who works with her part time, Dad— Matt Zapalski—is in charge of the chives and English thyme. Mary Konopka, a friend Marilyn has gardened with for more than a decade, is responsible for taking a weekly herb load to . . . market for Saturday morning selling. She also has several employees. . . .

"It's encouraging to see more people—people without ethnic ties to have started them out—are cooking creatively," she says.

From the first printed cookery book . . .

"Platina, De honesta voluptate"
aka

"A little work on foods and honest indulgence by the very learned man Platina: Printed in Venice with the work and care of Father Larentius of Aquila and also Sibyllinus Umber for the distinguished Duke Peter Mocenicus. On the Ides of June, 1475."

"On Basil"

What the Greeks call OKIMON, we for a long time have also called OCYMUM. I believe that it is commonly known as BA-SILICON. It is sown in Spring, and planted in Summer when it grows better from a slip. It blooms first at the bottom and then at the top (as Theophrastus says) and remains in bloom a long time. Chrysippus, the physician, attributes harmful effects to BASIL, saying that it is not good for the stomach, it dulls the eyes, brings on madness, obstructs the liver and, for these reasons, even the goat never touches this kind of herb.

Moreover, if it is pounded and covered up with the same stone, scorpions are produced. When mashed up and put in the sun, it makes worms, and it is said to nourish lice. Africans also think it is a fact that if one is stung by a scorpion and has eaten BASIL on the same day, he cannot be cured.

Actually, all these things have been found to be false. For goats do eat BASIL and man does not lose his reason by smelling it and, mixed with wine and vinegar, it heals stings of scorpions, either the land or sea varieties. In addition, this use has been discovered, that when it is mixed with vinegar and inhaled by the faint, it is strengthening. Galienus states that the scorpion is so fond of the odor of BASIL that it therefore willingly comes near the stalk. Nevertheless, it should be taken in small quantities, because it is quite potent on account of its warmth.

Translated into English from the Renaissance Latin by Elizabeth Buermann Andrews, Volume V from the Mallinckrodt collection of Food Classics, 1967, copyrighted by the Mallinckrodt Chemical Works. (Emphasis added.)

A Fox Hill Farmer's Note:

This book is not a learned exposition on *Ocimum basilicum* (sweet basil's botanical name).

Instead, it is a practical guide to the many uses of this marvelous herb and its many varieties, including recipes, how-to-grow-it information, preservation techniques and more.

2

*T*he Basil Brothers:

Personality Profiles

Basil's Many Faces

*T*here are 150 species of basil worldwide. So it's not at all unusual to find chefs around the globe using different kinds of basil but referring to them by the same common name . . . just plain old "basil" in whatever language or dialect that's prevalent.

Here's a quick linguistic guide to asking for basil:

English:	basil
French:	basilic commun
Italian:	basilico
Greek:	vasiliko
Thai:	ka prou
German:	das basilienkraut
Danish/Norwegian:	basilikum
Spanish:	albahaca

One old folk tale warns that evil will befall basil lovers if they dare to harvest basil before the first cutting is made by the king with his special golden sword.

And, botanically speaking . . .

Botanists have their own language. That language assures uniformity, meaning that no matter where in the world you might be, a particular plant has only one name which consists of:

a genus name (like a last name or family name),

a species name (similar to a first name)

and a variety or cultivar name (similar to a middle name or a nickname).

The familiar sweet basil's botanical name is

Ocimum (Genus) *basilicum* (species)

So, if you're in Greece and can't remember *vasiliko,* just say, "*Ocimum basilicum,* please!"

Of the 150 species of basils *(Ocimi)* that botanists have identified, only about four species generate the many basil varieties that are economically or historically important.

The Basil Personality Profiles will focus on those varieties that are good to eat or fun to do other things with. We'll leave the rest of the basil bunch to the botanists.

Genealogically speaking . . .

Even basil has a botanical family tree that takes root in the earliest crack of evolution. Oh so slowly as the earth evolved, did basil evolve along with all other plant and animal life.

Basil belongs to the greater plant family of the *Labiatae*.

This group of plants includes most of the culinary herbs, and they usually have one physical characteristic in common: they have square stems. Lemon balm, catnip, bergamots, sages, the mints, the thymes, the savories, rosemaries, marjorams and the oreganos adorn that *Labiatae* family tree along with all of the basil bunch.

Making Sense of Basil's Scents

When a chef says "basil," in whatever language, which of the basil brothers does he really mean? He may not know the botanical name or even the expanded common name, but a cook's nose knows the basil brother required for his cuisine.

The basil brothers contain essential oils that give them their characteristic fragrances. In most instances, there is a distinct fragrance and flavor difference between the various species and varieties of basil. And there can even be a flavor difference between the leaves, the flowers and the seed!

(Although dill is not a basil brother, dill does best demonstrate the different flavors that can be produced by one plant. Go ahead, find out for yourself. There is a significantly different flavor found in dill weed (the green leaves), dill seed (which to me tastes like caraway) and the sweetness of the dill flower. In addition to the brine, this difference is a major factor in flavoring dill pickles.)

But, back to basil now.

The essential oils of each species and variety are composed of different mixtures of the alcohols, terpenes, aldehydes, ketones and phenols that together make the basil brothers and cousins so similar yet so different.

The Basil Cousins Flavor Components chart graphically depicts the flavor ingredients of sweet basil, lemon basil and holy basil.

Flavor Components of the Basil Cousins

Flavor Name	Chemical Name	Sweet O.basilicum	Lemon O.americanum	Holy O.sanctum
Anise	methyl chavicol	x		x
Camphor	camphor		x	
Cinnamon	methyl cinnimate		x	
Clove	eugenol	x		x
Lemon	citral		x	x
Rose	geranial			
Sweet, flower	linalool	x		x
Thyme	thymol			

Sweet Basil
(Ocimum basilicum)

The basic basil. Sweet basil is a voluptuous, robust strong-growing character, with a wide reputation in folklore as well as in culinary use.

Plant description: The sweet basil bush grows about 2 to 3 feet tall, depending on environmental factors. The plant branches readily at almost every leaf node and thus has a fairly open skeleton of square stems growing from a solitary trunk.

As the plant ages, the square succulent stems and trunk are replaced by the woody structure typical of a shrub. Indeed, in mild temperate climates where sweet basil is hardy, it is a semi-woody shrub.

Sweet basil's leaf is a bright, shiny, deep green with a glistening, smooth surface. Leaf edges (margins) may be smooth or slightly toothed (serrated). In midsummer, the leaves are frequently 3 inches long and 2 inches wide and sometimes even larger, with a leaf petiole about 1 inch long.

The flowering spikes (inflorescences) of sweet basil are filled with many whorls of white petaled florets. Sometimes, the anthers are a bright orange color, but usually they are white.

Sweet basil seed is nearly round, small (1.0×1.5mm) and so dark brown to be almost black in color. The seed is ripe in late September when it falls or is shaken out of the calyxes (the green capsule that holds the floret petals in place).

Flavor: Sweet basil can have a broad range of flavors depending on the strain of the seed and the cultural/environmental conditions under which it is grown. The flavor is best described as stimulating, with a complex aroma that is at once pungent, sweet, clove-like, anise-like with a hint of mint.

Origin: Most likely, sweet basil originated in India and/or Thailand and emigrated west to Babylon with early traders.

A Fox Hill Farmer's Note:

Botanists classify sweet basil as an annual, meaning that its life cycle is terminated once it sets seeds. Our experience is that sweet basil can be kept alive and vital for many seasons with routine pruning. Hence, we consider it a very tender perennial.

Propagation: Sweet basil seed germinates readily in two to three days in warm conditions (70–75 degrees Fahrenheit). It is also very easy to propagate from stem cuttings taken from firm wood. Sweet basil seed holds its germinating capacity for several years if stored under favorable conditions.

Use: Sweet basil is primarily used in cooking. But it is also used for medicinal purposes, in toiletries, as an insect repellant and in folklore it has a significant reputation as an aphrodisiac, a burial herb and in other spiritual/religious/occult/mystical/ superstitious practices.

> . . . Name your love and there lies basil's erotic power;
> . . . Name your otherworldly fears and there, too, lies basil, lurking demon-like.

French Fine Leaf Basil
(Ocimum basilicum minimum var.)

The dainty French fine leaf basil is beloved by the cooks of Southern France. Many a kitchen doorstep is adorned with a potted plant that provides quick sprigs for the cook.

Plant description: The French fine-leaf basil is characterized by its thousands of tiny leaves. The bright green leaves are smooth surfaced with smooth leaf margins. They measure $1/8$ inch by $1/4$ inch in size. The plant branches freely on an open structure, growing to 2 feet tall and 18 inches wide. Sometimes, the branches lose their typical squareness and become somewhat flattened and convoluted, looking like they belong on some other plant! The white florets that grace the flowering inflorescences are typically arranged in whorls of six florets spaced along the flowering spike which can contain seven to ten floral whorls.

Flavor: A sweet, flowery, minty undertone can be detected in the complex flavor of the French fine leaf basil. It seems to be lacking in the acidic backbite sometimes characteristic of sweet basil.

Propagation: The black seed germinates readily in three to five days at about 75 degrees Fahrenheit with no particular problems. The French fine-leaf basil also propagates readily from cuttings.

Use: Use in salads as a green, in light butter and cream sauces, in broths and as a garnish, as well as in turtle soup. Its delicate flavor does not hold up long over high cooking heat. French fine leaf basil is also said to repel flies.

A Fox Hill Farmer's Note:

We find the French fine leaf basil to be a tender perennial suited to pot culture. When it is well maintained—pruned and repotted regularly—the plant will live for years. The wood, however, is very brittle and care must be taken so that the plant does not split. Staking and tying the lower part of the main trunk will help support it.

This is also one of the hardier basils. It regularly exhibits about four to six degrees more frost tolerance than other *Ocimum basilicum* varieties.

Lettuce Leaf Basil
(Ocimum basilicum crispum)

So curly, it reminds you of leaf lettuce, that's lettuce leaf basil.

Plant description: Lettuce leaf basil is a short, squat plant. Its many-branched, compact skeletal structure is adorned with very large leaves, which measure 5 inches long by 4 inches wide, and larger. The leaves are a mid-green, shiny, with a slight serration along the leaf margin.

The most outstanding characteristic about lettuce leaf basil is its three dimensionality. The leaf surfaces are wavy, almost puckered, as if someone threaded the leaf margins, then pulled the thread to develop a regular puckering. This, in turn, also causes the leaves to be gracefully convex, reminiscent of savoy cabbage and a frilly leaf lettuce. There are several patterns of puckering and cupping, as lettuce leaf basil is a very variable plant, morphologically speaking.

Origin: The Far East, possibly Japan.

Propagation: Lettuce leaf basil germinates readily from seed in about five to seven days at 75 degrees. It is prone to damp-off disease so special attention should be given to growing medium sterility and ventilation. Lettuce leaf basil does not propagate readily from cuttings.

Use: Lettuce leaf basil can be used interchangeably with sweet basil. Because of its leaf texture, it is especially nice as a salad green and a finger food wrapper.

Dark Opal Basil
(Ocimum basilicum purpurascens var "dark opal")

The deep purple color is so vivid, many people grow dark opal basil as an ornamental plant, never knowing the flavor it possesses.

Plant description: Dark opal basil grows about 12 to 15 inches tall and 12 inches wide. Like the other basils, it branches at the leaf nodes, and branching is stimulated by pruning the terminal leaf cluster.

The beautiful, jewel-like purple tones of its color are the brightest at the tips of its branches, especially in the top two to three leaf clusters. Leaf clusters further down the stems are less intense in color and tend to be somewhat mottled.

Dark opal basil leaves measure 2½ inches long by 2 inches wide. They are almost wedged shaped and have a marked ser-

ration on the leaf margins. Pairs of leaves adorn the square
stems at alternating angles, leading to the flowering spike.

The florets composing the flowering spike are a deep pink in
color, with purple calyxes holding the florets in place. The
spike is shorter than that of other *Ocimum basilicum* cultivars;
it is usually composed of about six to eight whorls of four to
six florets per whorl. Dark opal basil acts more like an annual
than any of the other basils; its tendency is to terminate its
own life cycle after pollination and seed development.

Flavor: Dark opal has a very full-bodied, complex flavor,
with a sweet spiciness not characteristic of sweet basil.

Origin: The striking dark opal basil cultivar was developed
at the University of Connecticut in the late 1950's. Its hand-
someness earned it the coveted All American Awards title.

Propagation: Grow dark opal basil from seed. It is finicky
and the most susceptible of all the basils to damp-off disease
and other fungus diseases. It also has a significantly lower germination rate than the other basil varieties, no matter how
fresh the seed is. Dark opal basil is not satisfactorily propagated from cuttings as there is a larger cuttings loss; it seems to
be resistant to rooting, and cuttings frequently rot. In addition,
plants grown from cuttings tend to flower fast, which in-
creases their maintenance requirements in the garden or pot.

Use: Dark opal basil marries nicely with heavier butter- or
cream-based sauces, dark meats, roasts and stews. It lends
beautiful color and bouquet to salad dressing vinegar. Use it
also as a salad green and in stir-fries.

A Fox Hill Farmer's Note:

Good dark opal basil seed produces a large proportion of
evenly colored purple plants. Poor seed produces a lot of
mottled plants, some sporting back to solid green. But, the
diet and growing conditions given to this basil can significantly affect its color.

Piccolo Verde Fino Basil
(*Ocimum basilicum var. "piccolo"*)

This basil is reputed to be the true, authentic pesto basil. Its sweetness is outstanding.

Plant description: Piccolo verde fino is a tall, strong-growing basil with a pronounced lust for life, growing to about 2½ feet tall and 2 feet wide on a loosely branched open structure. Its leaves are a bright, glossy, true green, somewhat narrow, measuring 2 inches long by 1¼ inches wide, with few marginal serrations.

Flavor: Piccolo's flavor is indeed reminiscent of a happy flute—light, lively, definitely sweet with a touch of anise and flowers. The flavor is very much up front on the palate, unlike the slowly unwinding complexity of some of the other basil varieties.

Origin: Probably a cultivar that developed in Europe.

Propagation: Grow piccolo from its dark brown to black seed or from cuttings; it's easy and reliable either way. Germinate the seed at about 70 degrees and you'll see a response in about three to five days. Cuttings root in seven to fourteen days, depending on the ripeness of the stem's wood and the time of the year.

Use: Try making your next batch of pesto with piccolo verde fino. Chop it coarsely for stir-fries and add it at the last minute. Perfume a soup with piccolo, but don't expose it to high heat of prolonged cooking, as that will devastate its up-front flavor.

Lemon Basil
(Ocimum americanum:
Ocimum canum × *Ocimum b.v. purpurascens)*

Almost more lemon-like than lemon is the sweet citrus flavor of the aptly named lemon basil.

Plant description: Lemon basil grows about 2 feet tall and 2 feet wide. It is an open, loosely branched plant with stems having a narrow diameter. The flowering spikes are long and lax with nine to twelve whorls of white petaled florets. The leaves of lemon basil are a dull gray-green, slightly fuzzy in texture and twice as long as they are wide: 2½ inches long by 1¼ inches wide. The leaf margins are almost entirely smooth, with just a slight undulating serration evident.

Flavor: A sweet lemony aroma almost overshadows the typical basil taste. Lemon basil is indeed a great pretender.

Origin: A fortuitous marriage between *O. canum* of Kenya and South Africa and *O. b.v. purpurascens* of Northwestern India, produced lemon basil, a well-documented natural hybrid. It is botanically unusual in that the hybrid, *O. americanum,* breeds true from seed, atypical of most other hybrids.

Propagation: Lemon basil is best propagated from seed which germinates well at 70–75 degrees Fahrenheit. Plants grown from cuttings tend to be awkward and overly floriferous, making them harder to maintain.

Use: Try this sweet lemon flavor in sauces for fish dishes, or simply stuff the cavity of a whole fish with a handful of lemon basil prior to poaching. It's also nice in a gooseberry or currant glaze and stir-fried with young shelled peas in sweet butter.

Thrysiflora Basil
(Ocimum basilicum var. "thrysiflora")

A basil bush with a flat-top look, decked out with pyramidal purple flowers.

Plant description: This basil has an overall pyramidal look to the plant and its flowering spike. The lower branches grow almost to the height of the main stem before starting secondary branching so that the plant is broader at the top than it is at soil level. The leaves are a sleek, elongated, mid-green with even, regular serrations on the leaf margin and measure three inches by one and one half inches.

Flavor: This is a basil for the sweet tooth. Its sweetness is almost overpowering.

Origin: India or Pakistan.

Propagation: No problem in growing this basil from seed or cuttings.

Use: Use it in floral bouquets as well as in cooking. Thrysiflora basil is also used in Thai cooking.

Nano Compatto Vero Basil
(Ocimum basilicum var. minimum cultivar)

Trim and pert and well groomed, this dainty, tiny-leaved basil is a knockout in the garden.

Plant description: Nano compatto vero basil is a jade green little bush growing 12 to 15 inches tall and equally as wide. It has a neat, compact growth habit with short, firm flowering spikes. The leaves measure ¼ inch long by ⅛ inch wide and are numerous. Leaf nodes are closely spaced, and branches grow from almost every one of them. The tiny seed is black.

Flavor: Nano compatto vero basil tends to have a fairly strong anise-clove undertone to its flavor.

Origin: Probably a cultivar developed in Europe.

Propagation: Nano compatto vero basil germinates readily from seed at about 70 degrees Fahrenheit and is also easy to propagate from cuttings.

Use: Nano sprigs make a nice garnish. Toss terminal bud leaf clusters into salads or use them in cheese and egg dishes and vegetable gratins.

Camphor Basil
(Ocimum kilimandscharicum)

Its fragrance reminds you of grandma!

Plant description: Camphor basil is a woody shrub growing about 3½ feet to 4 feet tall. The branching is open and loose. The leaves are about 3 inches by 1 inch, serrated and hairy, and their light to gray-green color lacks sweet basil's sheen. The leaves frequently fold on their midribs. The flowering stalks of camphor basil tend to be a foot long, with many white florets containing orange-red anthers.

Fragrance: Camphor basil is not considered a culinary herb. It has a very distinctive camphor aroma.

Origin: Camphor basil is native to East Africa.

Propagation: Camphor basil is best propagated from firm cuttings. Its seed, which is difficult to obtain, is shiny, black, pitted and slightly ridged with a marked camphor odor and germinates in three to five days.

Use: Because of a 70–80 percent camphorata content, camphor basil's oil is an important source of camphor and is primarily used medicinally. Camphor basil can also be used in moth-repelling herb blends for natural fabric storage.

Licorice Basil
(Ocimum basilicum var. "licorice")

What looks like piccolo verde fino, with flowers the color of holy basil and a taste somewhat like French tarragon? You guessed it—licorice basil.

Plant description: This is a very open-branched basil with long internodes. Licorice basil grows 2 to 2½ feet tall and about 1½ feet in diameter. The plant has an open look to it because of the long internodes. The leaves are shiny, yet give the impression of a matte finish, slender and pointed. They measure about 2 to 3 inches long by 1 to 1½ inches wide and have an almost purple case to the veining. The florets and calyxes also show a slight purple cast.

Origin: India and Pakistan, and possibly Thailand.

Propagation: Licorice basil germinates readily from seed and also is easy to propagate from cuttings taken on firm wood.

Use: Licorice basil is a nice addition to fruit salads and poultry. Its distinctive fragrance can be showcased in potpourri.

Cinnamon Basil
(Ocimum basilicum cv. "cinnamon"*)*

Cinnamon basil looks like licorice basil but has a flavor reminiscent of a breakfast roll.

Plant description: A nicely shaped large plant, growing to 2 feet tall, cinnamon basil has a full, bushy look to it. Its somewhat rounded, bright green, glossy leaves are topped with flowering spikes adorned with lavender florets. The leaves are mid-sized, measuring 3 inches long by 1¾ inches wide.

Flavor: A sweet cinnamon spicy taste with mild undertones of cloves.

Origin: Probably Northern India, but it may be a naturally occurring cultivar developed by selective breeding in Europe.

Propagation: Cinnamon basil seed germinates readily at 70 degrees Fahrenheit and is easily propagated from soft wood cuttings.

Use: The sweet, candy-like spice of cinnamon basil is right at home in desserts and with other dishes that have a sweetness to them. Try it with rhubarb too.

Bush Basil
(Ocimum basilicum minimum)

Bush basil looks just like a miniature fluffy bush.

Plant description: Growing about 18 inches tall, and to a similar girth, bush basil is fitted out with thousands of ½-inch leaves. The leaves are a bright, shiny green, almost round in shape, with a slight serration along the tip end of the leaf. The bush is compact and many branched with the typical white florets on fairly long inflorescences.

Flavor: A mild clove-like flavor with a touch of sweetness characterizes the bush basil.

Origin: Native to India, bush basil was introduced to Europe about 1563 and now grows lustily on the Mediterranean coast as well as in many U.S. gardens.

Propagation: The bush basil seed is dark brown to black in color and almost round in shape. It tends to fall at the small end of the basil seed size spectrum. Bush basil seed germinates readily in three to five days at 75 degrees with no major germination problems. Bush basil propagates readily from firm softwood cuttings.

Use: Use interchangeably with French fine leaf basil or nano compatto vero basil. Add during the last few minutes of cooking.

"Tulasi" Holy Basil
(Ocimum sanctum)

Plant description: Holy basil is a tall, open plant. Some varieties have green and others have purple foliage. The plants grow to 2 feet tall and are loosely branched. The flowering spikes hold pink to purple florets. The leaf is mid-sized, ovoid to elongated, with some marked leaf serration. The purple krishna's leaves are green on the underside. The stems are hairy.

Flavor: Sweetly spicy with a sharp, pronounced clove scent and pungency.

Origin: India, Micronesia.

Propagation: Holy basil germinates readily from seed with no special problems. Plants grown from cuttings flower too readily.

Use: Tulasi is revered and has use in the religious ceremonies of several Hindu and Muslim religious sects, including the Hare Krishna who offer the holy basil to Vishnu. In Western cultures, its rich sweetness is appropriate for fruit dishes, sweet yeast breads, jellies and preserves as well as for potpourris, sachets and fragrant toiletries.

Genovese Basil
(Ocimum basilicum var. "Genovese")

A beautiful harlequin of sleek green and deep purple.

Plant description: This sweet basil cultivar grows about 1½ feet tall on an open plant bedecked with bi-colored leaves and topped with purple flowering spikes. The coloration of the leaves is very variable from plant to plant; some plants show the purple color only in the leaf midribs, and other plants have leaves that are almost completely purple. The leaves are near ovoid in shape, measuring about three inches long and two inches wide with minimal leaf edge serration. The seed is black. The flowering spikes are compact rather than elongated, with purple florets presented in purple calyxes.

Flavor: The typical sweet basil flavor with an anise and clove accent.

Origin: Unknown.

Propagation: Grow Genovese basil from seed, which germinates readily at 70 degrees Fahrenheit, or from cuttings which root readily. Propagate from cuttings to reproduce your favorite colorations. Watch for damp-off in propagation.

Use: Use Genovese in tomato-based dishes, as a salad green and in floral bouquets as well as in potpourris and sachets.

3

The Oh Boy, BASIL! Festivals

After delivering many, many pounds of fresh sweet basil to chef Jimmy Schmidt at Detroit's London Chop House, we faced a long, cold drive home in the trusty, but very rusty, Fox Hill Farm truck. The haunting fragrance of its precious cargo still hung in the frosty air. Ah, sweet basil. A little moonlight, a little madness and another sixty-five miles to home.

In the cold of the February midnight, the imagined warmth of midsummer felt good. It would be our tenth year in existence, and we began to think of what we could do to celebrate. The traditional open house would not quite fit the bill. It would have to be a very special event. It would have to be fun.

It would help Fox Hill say "thanks" to all the people who helped us over the years. It would have seminars. It would run like clockwork. It would have a basil-laden buffet. And we would have a pesto-making competition, the Pesto Challenge, to determine . . .

WHO'S THE BEST PESTO MAKER IN THE LAND?

And to get folks in the mood, we would ask them to submit, along with their registration forms

254, MORE OR LESS, WORDS ABOUT BASIL
(OR A PICTURE WILL DO IN A PINCH)

Thus, on a winter's night, the Oh Boy, BASIL! Festival was born. And life has not been the same since.

How To Cook Over 100 Pounds Of Linguini, Al Dente, On Two Antique Laundry Stoves And
How To Process Enough Pesto To Sauce Over 100 Pounds Of Linguini

One of the advantages of having no commercial food experience and believing that nothing is impossible (having read *The Little Engine That Could* too frequently as a child) is that it never occurs to you that something cannot or should not be done. And as for the practical realities of getting it done right. . . .

You can look it up in Mrs. Beaton or Fannie Farmer or any other cookbook. And you too will find no firm guidance, no hard and fast rules, distilled from the brow of an expert.

So, dear readers, don't do as we did and forge blithely forth with kettles at full boil and basil, cheese and oil at the ready. Get it catered instead.

Or, better yet, invite our sophisticated friend, ad agency executive and "Food Enthusiast" newsletter publisher, Molly Hudson, to bring her own food processor and her husband to whip up a quick ten gallons of pesto sauce. Of course, we did have to give her some directions: a fresh batch of pesto sauce for every two pounds of linguini, cooked at six-minute intervals. After two basil festival performances, Molly's gotten smart and moved to the East Coast, where she too will tend a few herbs and pursue a dual career.

Chicago Tribune
August 11, 1982

On a Sunday afternoon in August, the bucolic quiet of a tiny town in the heart of Michigan's flat farming land was broken by the arrival of nearly 500 people who came to celebrate an herb. . . .

Perhaps the most stirring event was the Pesto Challenge. This contest tested one's wits. Among the seven stoves lined up at the edge of seven picnic tables were old-fashioned, gas-fired laundry spiders that dated from the early 1900s when every farmhouse kept one in the basement to heat the wash water. . . .

Marilyn Hampstead, owner of Fox Hill Farm . . . allowed that "just finding the equipment was almost a treasure hunt." One week before the festival she had found only four spiders and two didn't work. . . .

She wanted to marinate 300 pounds of boneless beef rounds for the dinner and talked the local—and only—grocery store in town into letting her use its cold locker. But not before having to get permission from the Michigan Department of Agriculture and the county Board of Health. Two weeks before the festival, the store burned down. In a flash of inspiration, she thought of Donna's bar in midtown Parma. It had a cold storage room holding but five kegs of beer. . . .

Then there was the little problem of getting enough basil for the meal and the contest. "I planned to pull one-half acre out of corn and replace it with basil, but first we did a soil test—and thank God we did. . . . We were six weeks from the festival and no extra basil." She cleared out one greenhouse and used every square inch. . . .

Nineteen pounds of basil were used for the contest alone.

And . . . The Winners!

The Best Pesto-makers In The Land Are:

DOLLIE SINELLI – 1982

Detroit Free Press,
August 11, 1982

Some 500 basil lovers made their way out to Fox Hill Farm near Parma recently to take part in the first annual Basil Festival. The highlight of the afternoon was the Pesto Challenge, a pesto–cook-off contest. Scores of pesto fans clustered around the tables and stoves in the open-air Pesto Challenge Pavillion (Piazza) to watch and taste as 19 contestants vied for the title of Best Pesto Maker in the Land.

. . . Ten years ago, most (American) people hadn't heard of pesto, and those who had didn't necessarily think it was such a big deal . . .

Pesto is of Italian extrac-

tion, and the Piemontese Social Club of Farmington Hills, whose members come from northwest Italy, was represented in force at the festival. . . . Pesto is really from Genoa, not Piedmont, one member was quick to explain, but the two regions are close together, and pesto is popular in both. . . .

When it was all over, the Piemontese pesto-makers walked away with three of the top five prizes, including first place. Dollie Sinelli . . . took top honors with a classic pesto recipe of basil, parsley, garlic, olive oil, butter, salt and pepper.

PESTO

1 lb. linguini
4 cups basil leaves (loosely
   packed)
½ cup curly parsley
2–3 cloves garlic, peeled

½ cup Parmesan cheese, freshly
   grated
¾ cup olive oil
4 tbs. butter

Place all ingredients (except linguini and cheese) in a food processor and process to a fine chop. Cook and drain linguini. In a serving dish, add a little butter to the linguini. Toss in half of pesto and ¼ cup cheese. Add balance of each and toss again.

No nuts.

Serves 4–6

COLLETTE WISMER–1983

Dayton Journal Herald
August 3, 1983

The contenders for the title of best pesto makers in the land took turns preparing their sauce . . . under the hungry eyes of people lined up for the food being served in the next tent.

Some used food processors; others used blenders and one or two used the traditional mortar and pestle. Some used pine nuts. Others added walnuts or almonds. Olive oils varied from supermarket oils such as Progresso and Filipp Berio to the fruitier Italian varieties. Some contenders added slightly untraditional touches such as the grated peel of a lemon. They varied their choices of basil. Some wanted sweet basil, others chose bush basil or piccolo verde fino.

At the end of the day the judges decided the best was turned out by Colette Wismer of St. Joseph, Mich.

Undaunted by severe thunderstorms and torrential rain, Colette Wismer traveled from St. Joseph, Michigan, to compete in the Pesto Challenge. Mother Nature smiled on her and the rain stopped pouring Sunday morning.

And how did Colette do it? Here's her winning recipe:

PESTO ALLA GENOVESE

2 cups fresh sweet basil leaves
1 cup Italian (flat) parsley
½ cup Asiago cheese, grated
½ cup Romano cheese, grated
12 almonds, blanched

1 tbs. pine nuts
12 walnuts, blanched
2 cloves garlic, peeled
3 tbs. butter, softened
½ cup olive oil

Place all ingredients in the blender except the cheeses. Blend until fully mixed. Empty into a large bowl and stir in the cheeses.

Cook 1 lb. linguini "al dente." Drain, reserving 4 tablespoons of the cooking water. Pour pasta right into the pesto. Toss well. Add the reserved hot water and toss again.   *Serves 4–6*

Dolly and Colette's pestos and the eight other prizewinning recipes that follow reflect America's changing palate and emerging technology. As Americans wean themselves from European cuisines, they are developing the self-confidence to create unique new food styles. Their springboards are classic, ethnic cuisines, revised with sometimes surprising regional, seasonal ingredients. This innovative flair is evident in even the simplest cooking competitions, like the Pesto Challenge.

We've also noticed that American cooks are quick to incorporate the latest technology into their technique. Classically, pesto is ground to a smooth paste by hand. In two years of competition only one Pesto Challenger chose the mortar and pestle to prepare his entry—Denniston Brown of Jackson, Michigan, who won third place in 1982. All other contestants have used numerous brands of food processors and blenders.

We present, for your delectation, the second-through-fifth-place-winning Pesto Challenge recipes as prepared in the Pesto Challenge Piazza at Fox Hill Farm. Since the winners hastily scribbled their secrets on scraps of paper and note cards after the competition, we've taken the liberty of clarifying those that may seem confusing to the beginner.

What Did the Pesto Challenge Winners Win?

1st Prize—$50 cash in a trophy topped with basil and a full pound of fresh cut basil each month for a year

2nd Prize—$25 cash in a trophy topped with basil and a half pound of fresh cut basil each month for a year

3rd, 4th and 5th Prizes—$10 cash in a trophy topped with basil and a half pound of fresh cut basil for six months

(cash prizes were in silver dollars)

LINDA BRUNAMONTI—2ND PLACE, 1982

2 cups fresh basil	1 tsp. salt, ½ tsp. pepper
1 cup parsley	½ cup Parmesan cheese, grated
4 cloves garlic, peeled	½ cup toasted pine nuts
¾ cup olive oil	

Blend basil and parsley in food processor. Add garlic while running, then olive oil. Stop. Add salt, pepper and Parmesan. Stir.

Cook 1 lb. pasta in salted water to al dente. Drain, put into serving container and add enough oil to coat. Pour pesto sauce onto pasta. Garnish with pine nuts. *Serves 4–6*

DENNISTON BROWN—3RD PLACE, 1982

2 cups basil leaves, loosely packed	2 cloves garlic, peeled
¾ cup olive oil	1 tsp. salt
2 tbs. pine nuts, plus extra for garnish	½ cup Parmesan cheese, grated

Crush garlic and salt with mortar and pestle. Add basil and pine nuts and make a paste. Add olive oil and slowly mix into paste.

Combine 1 lb. cooked pasta with pesto sauce. Add Parmesan cheese and pine nuts to garnish. *Serves 4–6*

LILLIAN DEMAESTRI—4TH PLACE, 1982

2 cups chopped basil
3–4 cloves garlic, peeled and chopped
2 oz. olive oil
salt and pepper
1 cup chopped walnuts
½ cup grated Parmesan
¼ cup butter

Mix basil, garlic, olive oil, salt and pepper together. Add walnuts and mix. Cook and drain 1 lb. of pasta. Add sauce to pasta and toss, then add Parmesan and butter.   *Serves 4–6*

WANDA PIZZORNI—5TH PLACE, 1982

1 lb. linguini, cooked and drained
6 oz. basil leaves
1 clove garlic, peeled
1 cup Parmesan cheese, grated
½ cup olive oil
¼ cup butter
⅓ cup pine nuts
salt

Put basil, garlic, ½ cup Parmesan, pine nuts, oil and salt in food processor. Quickly process to a fine chop (not into paste). Cook linguini, drain, add butter and toss. Add pesto sauce, toss, add remaining cheese, toss and serve. *Serves 4–6*

RUTH OHLSEN—2ND PLACE, 1983

4 cups sweet basil leaves, lightly packed
3 garlic cloves, peeled
3 oz. Romano cheese, coarsely grated
5 oz. Parmesan cheese, coarsely grated
1 tsp. marjoram, dry
¼ cup pine nuts
5 walnuts
4 oz. olive oil, Bertoli
6 tbs. butter, salted
Lawry's lemon pepper and seasoned salt to taste

Cut garlic in the food processor. With the blade in motion, add basil leaves and continue to process. Add oil, 3 tablespoons butter, nuts, salt and pepper. Then add cheeses, pulsing the food processor.

Cook 1 lb. linguini al dente, drain, place in large bowl, add 3 tablespoons salted butter, then toss. Add pesto, toss again and serve.   *Serves 4–6*

KEVIN OLDHAM—3RD PLACE, 1983

2 cups firmly packed fresh basil leaves, washed
¼ cup roasted pine nuts
3 cloves garlic, peeled
1 cup freshly grated Parmesan cheese
½ cup olive oil

In a blender, puree basil, nuts and garlic. Mix in cheese. Slowly add oil while blending on a low speed.

1 lb. pasta
2 6½ oz. cans minced clams
2 tbs. lemon juice, fresh
1½ tsps. lemon rind, minced

Oldham gave no directions for the incorporation of the above ingredients. It's up to you!   *Serves 4–6*

SAM PALAZZOLO—4TH PLACE, 1983
(Sam was sick and had to stay home, so his recipe was prepared by Betty La Rocca and Maxine Hill.)

½ cup Berio Lucca olive oil
4 cups fresh basil leaves, stems removed
¼ cup fresh parsley, stems removed
4 medium cloves garlic, peeled and pressed
½ cup Leccotelli imported Romano cheese, grated
¼ cup coffee cream
½ cup freshly grated imported Parmesan cheese
1½ lbs. imported semolina spaghetti
¼ lb. butter

Pour olive oil in a blender, add pressed garlic and blend. Add parsley and slowly add basil leaves until all is blended. Pour into bowl, stir in grated cheeses and blend in coffee cream. (Omit coffee cream if you're going to freeze pesto sauce.) Cook pasta in boiling salted water, al dente. Drain, reserving some liquid. Add ½ to 1 stick butter (in pieces, until pasta is well coated). Gradually add pesto sauce. If too dry, add some of the reserved liquid.

Serve immediately on individual plates, topped with freshly grated Parmesan cheese. *Serves 6*

Hint: To freeze, double recipe, pour into ice tray (with dividers). When frozen, remove cubes and store in a plastic container. To defrost, allow one cube per person and keep at room temperature until soft, add cream, then add to hot spaghetti and serve.

DEBORAH VANDERBROEK—5TH PLACE, 1983

2 cups basil leaves, stripped from
   their stems, chopped and
   tightly packed
1 tsp. salt
½ tsp. freshly ground black
   pepper

6 large cloves garlic, peeled
2 tbs. finely chopped walnuts
1–1½ cups olive oil
½ cup freshly grated Parmesan
   cheese
2–3 tbs. unsalted butter

Combine chopped basil, salt, pepper, garlic, walnuts and 1 cup olive oil in a blender or food processor. Blend them at high speed until ingredients are smooth, stopping every five to six seconds to push herbs down with a spatula. The sauce should be thin enough to run off the spatula easily. If it seems too thick, blend in as much as ½ cup more olive oil. Transfer the sauce to a bowl and stir in grated cheese, or blend sauce with cheese in blender or food processor. Serve with 1 lb. cooked and drained pasta. *Serves 4–6*

Here's How They Get Into
the Basil Festival Spirit . . .

254, More or Less, Words About Basil

1982 WINNING ENTRY

MERRY AND JOE CHARTKOFF, EAST LANSING,
MICHIGAN

A Few Words About Basil

We first came to love pesto at precisely 8:30 P.M., July 29, 1976. That's local time at Spannocchia (Siena Prov.), Italy. Love struck quickly. It was our first meal in Italy when we first went there to do archaeology. Dinner started at 8:00 P.M. sharp, and it was 8:30 when we actually began eating the first course, plates of pesto.

The visual reaction lasts as strongly as the taste sensation. The mind still brings forth in sharp relief the sight of plates heaped with masses of meandering linguini, the whole overlaid with a thick stratum of green slime. An oily slick in which small bits of plant matter were suspended. To those of us with southern Italian backgrounds, the sight was unsettling, not at all a promising way to start a campaign of hard labor in foreign climes. Memories of dormitory food flooded forth—servings of Jello with strange leftovers suspended in the matrix.

But archaeologists must be hardy campaigners above all else, and we, after twenty-four hours of airplane food, were willing enough to give ground food of any sort a try. A few tentative probes, a mouthful, and it was love.

The tale began there but ended at distant times and places. We ended up back in Michigan in due course and brought with us the knowledge that our new love was known by the name of pesto. No summer romance, this; no one-night stand. We determined to recreate the entire experience in our own kitchen. We would have brought the recipe home, but the cook at Spannocchia was not entirely sure how she made the dish. But here in the land of ten thousand cookbooks, any door may be opened with a magic word, and the word "pesto" brought us more recipes than we would deal with.

We tried recipes and recipes. They weren't awful, but the magic just wasn't there. We compared notes; it wasn't the recipes but the ingredients. Next summer's trip came, and on the way home we lugged a five-liter tin of Tuscan olive oil. It was better; it gave us the distinctive green that we had come to cherish, and for which the pallid yellow stuff they sell here is useless. Better, but still not right, never quite true.

It was just three weeks ago, and this is the Lord's truth, that some friends happened to pass through Fox Hill Farm, heard about the basil festival, and while there, bought us a pot of Genovese basil. One sniff tells the difference between this magnificent herb and the pallid weeds grown from Burpee's offerings. But will it be the key? Will it be the last latch to open the door once again? We don't know. We have planted the basil and are nourishing it, trying to get it to flourish. But we will know soon. Soon enough.

1983 WINNING ENTRY
RACHEL BERRY, MIDLAND, MICHIGAN

A Basil By Any Other Name . . .

You can say bah-sil
or you can say bay-sil
but any way you say it
it's good on your table.
You can grow it in your garden,
you can grow it in a pot,
you can use it in your cooking
and it doesn't take a lot.
You can chop it,
     chomp it,
     freeze it,
     fricassee it,
        dry it,
        fry it,
            grate it and
            gyrate it.
Too bad it's unpronounceable,
it really is a shame,
but after all, dear Basil,
what the hell is in a name?

The Authentic Fox Hill Farm Pesto

THE ABRIDGED, WIDELY PUBLISHED, OFFICIAL RECIPE

4 cups basil leaves—Piccolo verde fino, sweet or fine leaf
¼ cup pine nuts or sunflower seeds (optional)
½ to ¾ cup olive oil
½ to ¾ cup Parmesan cheese, freshly grated
2 to 3 cloves garlic, peeled

In a food processor, fine chop pine nuts. Add garlic cloves and process to a fine chop. Add ½ the basil leaves and process very quickly to a coarse chop. Add balance of basil and process very quickly to a medium chop.

With processor running, slowly add oil, then cheese. Do not overprocess.

Cook 1 lb. pasta al dente, add ½ cup hot pasta water to pesto and process just to incorporate. Drain pasta.

Pour both hot pasta and pesto sauce thinned with pasta water into a large serving bowl. Toss and serve. *Serves 4–6*

But, Here's How We Really Do It

For mature cooks only. Taken from a letter to Mrs. Hugh Johnston.

THE COMPLETE UNEXPURGATED, UNOFFICIAL FOX HILL FARM PESTO RECIPE

Frieda, nobody's ever asked, but this is how I do it.

Put a large pasta pot of water on the stove over high heat, covered, with a little salt.

Take a standard size kitchen colander and go to the garden with a nice cold glass of wine and either kitchen scissors or strong fingernails, which are what I use. Take off your high-heeled shoes. Snip off enough three-joint long sweet basil leaf clusters to loosely fill the colander. If your garden is mulched, the basil may not even need to be washed and blotted dry.

The trick is to manage the colander and wine in one hand while you snip or pinch off the basil growing points with the other.

Back in the kitchen, snake 1 lb of vermicelli into the boiling water, uncovered, and set the kitchen timer for 4½ minutes.

Then, start the pesto sauce.

In a food processor or blender throw in a small handful of pine nuts or sunflower seeds, if they are handy. Process briefly. Add three cloves fresh garlic, process briefly. Pinch off the top tight four leaf cluster and bottom two leaves of the basil stems and loosely fill the processor bowl. Process very quickly to a coarse chop, about fifteen to twenty seconds. Fill the processor bowl with basil again and again process to coarse chop. With the processor running, pour ½ to ¾ cup olive oil and slowly pour in ¾ cup Parmesan cheese, more or less.

Add ½ cup hot pasta water and process very briefly. Remove sauce to a bowl.

The kitchen timer should ring right about now.

Drain pasta in a colander, shake colander briskly to remove excess water.

Toss pasta in the bowl with the sauce. Toss, savoring the aroma. Taste regularly and serve immediately.

A Fox Hill Farmer's Note:

A Bunch and a Pinch: They Defy Definition

There is little standarization within the fresh herb produce trade as to what a bunch is; it really differs from herb to herb. For instance, it may take only three 6 inch sprigs of sage or basil to make a bunch weighing over an ounce, but 25 to 30 leaf stalks of chervil make a big, half-ounce bunch. Usually there are 4 to 6 sprigs of sweet basil in a bunch and 8 to 10 sprigs of French fine leaf in a bunch. Nor does weight work as an adequate measure because at different times of the year, sprigs of the same plant, at the same length, will have different weight, depending upon how much calcium the plant has deposited in its stems.

Pinches differ based on the size of one's thumb and the texture of the substance being measured. So call a pinch ⅛ to ½ teaspoon.

But There's More to Basil Festivals than Food!

The Hysterical Basil

Jan Longone intrigues her audiences with tales of basil's sometimes gruesome exploits through history. And they especially warm up to her rendition of Keats's "Isabella; or the Pot of Basil," with high points like:

Our heroine Isabella's beau was murdered by her wicked brothers. She finds his head and buries it in a pot of basil which she keeps by her side day and night.

> . . . And so she ever fed it with thin tears,
> Whence thick and beautiful it grew,
> So that it smelt more balmy than its peers
> Of basil-tufts in Florence . . .

The plot thickens as Isabella's brothers then steal the pot of basil from her:

> O melancholy, turn thine eyes away!
> For Isabel, sweet Isabel, will die;
> Will die a death too lone and incomplete,
> Now they have taken away her basil sweet.
> . . . And so she pined, and so she died forlorn,
> Imploring for her basil to the last.
> No heart was there in Florence but did mourn
> In pity for her love so overcast.
> And a sad ditty of this story born
> From month to month through all the country passed:
> Still is the burthen sung—"O cruelty,
> To steal my basil-pot away from me!"

An authority on American cookery books, Longone operates the Wine and Food Library in Ann Arbor, Michigan. She's presented scholarly papers at Oxford University in London, serves on the advisory board of the American Institute of Wine and Food and also assembled from her collection the first major American cookery book exhibition.

And Basil Festival revelers clamor for more of her tales of basil!

Gardening with Basil

And no celebration of this notorious herb could be complete without solid instruction in the secrets of successful basil culture.

Syndicated garden writer Elvin McDonald's cultural command of the basils generates an uncommon synergy between man and herb—with breathtaking results. Would you believe topiary basils, for example?

From the roots on up, McDonald's depth of knowledge is telegraphed through the throngs; they get the drift of growth, and they are armed with solid ammunition to recreate the Basil Festival on their own.

As the Festival revelers depart, sated with basil, satisfied, Leota presents them with one final parting remembrance of the day: a commemorative potted basil plant to take home.

Even saints are named the same as this simple herb. In Greece, for instance, St. Basil's Day is cause to celebrate and give gifts as much as Christmas and Hanukkah. St. Basil ushers in the new year and epitomizes philanthropy. Look on the Julian calendar. June 14th is St. Basil's Day.

4

Basil in the Pot:

More Recipes
from the Basil Festivals

Jimmy Schmidt Wows 'Em with
His Delectable Dishes

Basil Festival participants sit in awed silence as this very talented young chef whips up imaginative cuisine in the rustic outdoor oak-bowered amphitheater. For good reason.

Jimmy's the pick of the culinary crop.

Trained by Madeleine Kamman in Boston, encouraged by the late Les and Cleo Gruber, Jimmy's innate food sense is enhanced by his creative spirit and contagious enthusiasm. In May 1983, Jimmy was one of ten chefs invited to prepare "An American Celebration" at the American Institute of Wine and Food's first fund-raising gala in San Francisco. Fox Hill Farm's bounty of native American seasonal foods like blanched dandelion crowns, wild mustard, cattail shoots, ground nuts and wild angelica (along with a heck of a lot of fresh-cut herbs) were shipped to him in San Francisco for the very successful extravaganza.

When he's not presenting basil cooking seminars, Jimmy's fare can be sampled daily at Detroit's famed London Chop House now owned by Max and Lanie Pincus.

An Ancient Recipe for Peas

1. Boil the peas. When the froth has been skimmed off put in leeks, coriander and cumin. Pound pepper, lovage, caraway, dill, fresh BASIL, moisten with liquamen, blend with wine and liquamen [add to the peas], bring to the boil. When it boils, stir. If something is wanting, add, then serve.

And classically speaking, the original Latin:

1. Pisam coques. cum despumaverit, porrum, coriandrum et cuminum supra mittis. Teres piper, ligusticum, [careum hoc est caravita] careum, anethum, OCIMUM VIRIDE, suffundis liquamen, vino et liquamine temperabis, facies ut ferveat. cum ferbuerit, agitabis. si quid defuerit, mittis et inferes.

Apicius, *The Roman Cookery Book,* translated by Barbara Flower and Elisabeth Rosenbaum, Peter Nevill Limited, London and New York, 1958, page 135.

A Simple, Elegant Three-course Dinner

Jackson Citizen Patriot,
August 4, 1982

A Basil Festival, Fox Hill style, is a cooking demonstration, seminars, a Pesto Challenge and an abundance of food, all liberally seasoned with basil. . . .

Three natives of Parma, Italy, were in the crowd. . . .

[They] said Parma, a city of 200,000, is the gastronomic capital of Italy. Parmesan cheese and prosciutto . . . are produced in that region. Parma, the birthplace of Toscanini and Verdi, is also known for its music, [they] said. . . .

The basil cooking demonstration was by Jimmy Schmidt, executive chef and general manager of the London Chop House at Detroit. He was assisted by four of his staff chefs.

"I'm doing a basil meal," Schmidt said to introduce his show. He and his crew poached a whole fryer, sauced trout fillets, marinated tomato salad, assembled pasta salad and whisked zabaglione, an Italian custard sauce for fruit, to perfection.

The French method, he said, was to poach a chicken in an animal's stomach. "The purpose is to keep the flavors in while it is cooking," Schmidt said. "I'm using a plastic bag." He pushed herb seasoned sweet butter under the skin of the chicken, dropped it in the bag with some julienne strips of onion and carrot, and sucked the air out of the bag. . . .

His method of skinning lake trout fillets was a crowd pleaser. "You can skin fish very easily." Schmidt demonstrated by placing a fillet, skin-side down, on a board and running a knife between the skin and the flesh from the tail toward the head.

He sauced the trout with a mixture of mayonnaise, lemon juice, olive oil, touches of mustard, salt and white wine, shallots, fresh basil and chives with egg yolk as a binder.

And, More of Jimmy's Basil Renditions Follow!

SPINACH FETTUCINI WITH PESTO AND ASPARAGUS

1 lb. fresh spinach pasta
½ cup fresh basil, chopped
2 tbs. garlic, chopped
¼ cup pine nuts, mashed
¼ cup olive oil
½ cup Pecorino Romano cheese, grated fine

¼ cup mushrooms, sliced
¼ cup cherry tomatoes, cut in half
1 bunch asparagus, peeled, blanched and sliced on the bias
2–4 lbs. whole sweet butter
salt and pepper to taste

Combine the basil, garlic, and pine nuts in a mortar and pestle. Work into a paste adding the olive oil as necessary. Slowly blend in the cheese and remaining olive oil. Reserve.

Prepare the vegetables. Reserve.

Cook the fettucini in a large amount of salted, boiling water. When just about al dente, combine the pesto with butter over medium heat and use this mixture to sauté the asparagus and mushrooms lightly. Add the drained pasta when al dente and toss. Add the cherry tomatoes. Add salt and pepper to taste. Serve immediately.   *Serves 4*

A Fox Hill Farmer's Note:

Rule of Thumb for Fresh vs Dry

1 tablespoon of fresh herbs = 1 teaspoon of dried.

When using fresh herbs, exact measurement is not critical; not measuring generally won't lead to bad results. However, using more than twice the volume of dried herbs called for in some recipes can be unsatisfactory. Most herbs, fresh or dried, should be added during the last 10 to 15 minutes of cooking to best present their flavors. Overlong cooking can kill some flavors while others will develop a bitter aftertaste. There are a lot of exceptions to this "rule." Greek oregano, bay leaf, thyme, winter savory and garlic hold up well through long cooking procedures. And don't forget that the leaves, soft stems and flowers all have flavor. Save the hard stems for the stock pot or for braising.

PÂTÉ DE POISSON

1 lb. scallops, cleaned
12 oysters, shucked
2 oz. salmon caviar
4 oz. salmon fillet, cleaned
2 egg whites
4 tbs. sweet butter
10 oz. whipping cream
salt and white pepper
½ bunch mint, chopped (about 3 tbs.)

1 bunch basil, chopped (about 6 tbs.)
8 oz. white wine (Chardonnay)
8 oz. white wine vinegar
4 oz. shallots, coarsely chopped
1 oz. white peppercorns
12 tbs. sweet butter
watercress for garnish

To prepare the pâté:

Preheat oven to 325 degrees.

Puree the scallops with the two egg whites until smooth. Reserve and chill.

With a mixer, whip 4 tablespoons butter with 1¼ teaspoons salt and ¼ teaspoon white pepper until smooth. Gradually add the scallop puree while whipping on high speed. Combine well until homogenous. On slow speed, slowly begin to add the whipping cream. As soon as all the cream has been added, proceed to a homogenous texture. Remove from the mixer. Gently fold in the mint and half of the basil. Then fold in the oysters and caviar.

Place half the pâté mix into a buttered terrine dish. Position the salmon fillet down the center. Cover with the remaining pâté mix. Smooth the top. Place buttered parchment directly on the surface of the pâté. Cover the parchment with foil.

Bake in a water bath at 325 degrees for approximately one hour. Test for doneness with a skewer.

To prepare the sauce:

In an acid-resistant pot, combine the white wine, white wine vinegar, shallots, and peppercorns. Reduce over high heat until just about nothing is left. Strain immediately and reserve.

Heat the sauce reduction to a rapid boil. Gradually whisk in the remaining 8 tablespoons butter. Season with salt and pepper. Continue to add the butter while reducing to sauce consistency. Remove from the heat and pour into a stainless bowl and whisk for a few seconds. Add the remaining basil and combine.

To serve, spoon the sauce onto the plate. Slice the pâté and place on top of the sauce. Garnish with watercress.   *Serves 4*

COLD ROAST LOIN OF VEAL
WITH BASIL SAUCE

1 loin of veal, 10 lbs., bone in	2 tbs. mustard
4 oz. olive or corn oil for sautéing	1 cup virgin olive oil
2 egg yolks	½ cup fresh sweet basil, chopped
1 lemon, juiced	salt and pepper to taste
	white wine as necessary

To prepare the veal loin:

With a boning knife, clean away all excess fat. Remove the single rib bone. Remove the sirloin and tenderloin by following the spinal bone structure from one end to the other. Gently work the eye away from the bone. Remove all connective and fat tissues. Reserve.

To prepare the basil sauce:

Combine the egg yolks, mustard and lemon juice in a mixing bowl. With the mixer on high, gradually add the olive oil. Lighten as necessary with white wine. Add the basil. Add salt and pepper to taste. Reserve.

To roast the veal:

Preheat the oven to 400 degrees. Sear the veal loin lightly in olive oil over medium high heat. When evenly seared, transfer to a roasting pan and roast for approximately ten to twelve minutes. Remove and allow to rest. (The veal should be medium rare.) Chill lightly.

When ready to serve, spoon the basil sauce onto a serving platter. Slice the veal across the grain very thinly. Fan the veal and place it on the basil sauce.

Garnish with fine leaf basil.   *Serves 10*

A Sampler of Some Other Jimmy Schmidt Basil Dishes

WALL STREET JOURNAL,
September 12, 1983

"For Trendy Diners, Basil is the Herb to be Seen With."

The ardor of basil devotees was illustrated by the scene at Parma, Mich., one weekend this summer. Seated on folding chairs in a grove of sky-high oaks, the crowd of hundreds watched in reverential silence as a chef prepared a dish called "salmon with basil beurre blanc." When it was completed and carried about for inspection, the disciples delivered a standing ovation.

What they were attending was a festival given over entirely to the herb of the hour; the "Oh Boy, BASIL!" festival, it was called. In attendance was Marge Linklater, who had driven over from Westland, Mich. "I wouldn't have come for sage," she said.

PAILLARD OF VEAL WITH PEPPERS AND BASIL

4 thin slices of veal from the leg, about 1 lb.
   remove all fat and connective tissues

Sauce:

8 tbs. olive oil
1½ cups mixed red and green peppers, decored, seeded and julienned
1 cup button mushrooms, sliced
2 cups heavy cream
½ cup veal stock
6–8 basil stems
¼ cup fresh basil, chopped fine
1 clove garlic, minced
1 lemon rind, grated

To prepare the fire:

Prepare a very hot charcoal fire. Place the grill as close to the hot coals as possible. Preheat the grill top at least fifteen minutes.

To prepare the veal:

With a meat bat, pound each slice of veal to just as thin as possible. Use some olive oil to help, if necessary. Reserve pounded veal.

To prepare the sauce:

Combine heavy cream, veal stock and basil stems in a sauce pot. Reduce to a light sauce consistency over medium heat. Strain and reserve.

Quickly sauté mushrooms and peppers over high heat. Add them to the reserved, strained sauce base. Reduce to a medium consistency. Adjust the seasonings. Remove from heat. Add the chopped basil, garlic and grated lemon rind. Stir and keep hot.

Sear, compose and serve:

Oil the paillards of veal. Lay slices on the grill without overlapping. Allow time for a good sear, only about one or two minutes.

Quickly turn slices over. Sear another thirty seconds or so to finish cooking the slices. Remove when just done. Do not overcook. (Cooking time is relative to grill temperature.)

Spoon the hot sauce onto a serving platter. Place the veal slices on the sauce. Put a little sauce over the veal. Garnish with a pretty sprig of fresh basil.   *Serves 4*

MEDALLIONS OF SALMON WITH BASIL BEURRE BLANC

1½ lbs. salmon fillet, skinned

Court Bouillon:
3 cups white wine vinegar
3 cups white wine
1 onion, coarsely chopped
2 oz. white peppercorns, whole
1 bay leaf
1 bunch fresh thyme (about twenty sprigs)

Sauce:
2 cups basil vinegar (or white wine vinegar)
1 cup shallots, coarsely chopped
2 oz. white peppercorns, whole
1 bunch (6–8) basil stems
½ lb. butter
1 cup mixed basil leaves—sweet, lemon and dark opal basil varieties—julienned

To prepare the court bouillon:
Combine the white wine vinegar, white wine, onion, peppercorns, bay leaf and thyme in an acid-resistant fish poacher. Add enough water to cover the fish. Simmer at least two hours before poaching fish.

To prepare the salmon medallions:
Cut the salmon fillets across the grain into equal sections, about 1 inch thick. Place two of the sections on a flat surface. Position the sections exactly opposite each other with the inner spine touching. Wrap one section around the other. Secure with two toothpicks through the end of each wrapped sections. Reserve.

To prepare the sauce:
Combine the white wine or basil vinegar, shallots, peppercorns and the basil stems in an acid-resistant saucepan. Reduce over high heat to about ¼ cup. Strain immediately and reserve.

Then, poach, compose and serve:
Place the salmon medallions into the simmering court bouillon. Reduce heat to prevent boiling. Simmer salmon me-

dallions about eight minutes. When done, quickly place medallions onto sauced serving platter, as indicated below.

Meanwhile, return sauce to a boil. Whisk 1 tablespoon of the butter at a time into the boiling sauce. Adjust seasonings. Reduce to a light sauce consistency.

Pour sauce into a stainless steel bowl and whisk for a few seconds to stabilize.

Spoon the sauce onto the serving platter. Sprinkle the julienne of basils evenly on top of the sauce.

Place the salmon medallions on top of the sauce. Garnish with a sprig of basil and serve. *Serves 4*

ROAST RIB OF YOUNG LAMB WITH BASIL

1 8–10 lbs. rack of lamb, aged

Stock:
1–10 lbs. veal bones
2–5 lbs. lamb bones
1 carrot
2 onions, coarsely cut

1 bunch parsley (8–12 stems)
3 bay leaves
4 tbs. whole black peppercorns
1 tb. thyme leaves

Wine Reduction:
1 bottle pinot noir red wine
1 onion, coarsely chopped
1 handful shallots, chopped
4 cloves garlic

1 oz. white peppercorns
1 bunch parsley stems
1 oz. juniper berries
1 oz. whole allspice

Sauce:
1 bunch fresh sweet basil (4–6 sprigs; separate leaves from stems and save both)
1 cup heavy cream

1 orange rind, grated
1 clove garlic, minced fine
4 tbs. sweet butter

Prepare the stock two days ahead:
Brown the stock bones in a 350-degree oven until golden. Place bones in a stock pot, discarding fat. Deglaze the roasting pan with a little water to rehydrate the carmelized pan juices. Add the juices to the stock pot. Add the remaining ingredients.

Cover with cold water and bring to a boil. Reduce heat and simmer for twenty-four to thirty hours. Replace the evaporated water as necessary. When finished, strain. Reserve the stock.

Then prepare the meat glaze:

Skim the fat from the stock. Place the stock over a medium to high heat. Bring it to a boil. Maintain a fast simmer allowing the stock to reduce until it lightly coats the back of a spoon. The resulting meat glaze will be about $\frac{1}{8}$ the original volume of the stock. Reserve.

And prepare the wine reduction:

Combine all the ingredients specified in an acid-resistant pot. Bring to a simmer. Reduce by $\frac{3}{4}$ of the original volume of the stock. Strain in a fine sieve. Reserve.

To roast the young lamb:

Have the two sets of ribs removed from the backbone. Trim the fat away from and between the rib bones extending from the eyes. Gently pull the fat away from the eyes without removing. Cover the exposed rib bones with aluminum foil. Reserve.

Preheat oven to 450 degrees.

First, place the lamb under the broiler for fifteen minutes. Remove from broiler. Trim the fat away that is covering the eyes. Return to the oven until the meat reaches the temperature desired for your own taste. 140 degrees medium rare, 145–150 degrees medium.

Remove from the oven and allow to rest.

Then prepare the sauce:

Add the basil stems to the cream. Reduce by half over medium-high heat. Strain and reserve.

Combine the wine reduction with 1 cup of the meat glaze. Bring to a fast simmer and allow to reduce back to 1 cup of light sauce consistency. Add the reduced cream and reduce back to a light sauce consistency. Reserve.

To present the lamb:

After the lamb has rested, return it to the broiler. Reheat toward your desired temperature.

Return the cream sauce to a simmer. Add the coarsely chopped fresh basil leaves, orange rind and minced garlic into the sauce. Whisk in the butter. Adjust the seasonings.

Spoon the sauce into the serving platter first. Then carve the meat off of the rib in long, thin slices. Arrange so that each slice slightly overlaps the previous slice. Spoon a touch of the sauce over the meat.

Garnish the platter with rosettes of fresh basil and serve. *Serves 8–10*

RAGOUT OF SHRIMP

20 shrimp, shelled and deveined
1 bunch French tarragon, destemmed (about ¼ cup)
1 lemon, juiced
1 head bibb lettuce, with large outer leaves
1 cup fish fumet
4 oz. white wine
8 oz. heavy cream

1 tsp. tomato paste
4 tbs. sweet butter
2 tbs. basil, chopped
1 clove garlic, minced
4 oz. diced fresh tomato
4 oz. white wine to steam with
4 oz. clam juice to steam with
salt and pepper

Remove twenty large outer leaves from the head of bibb lettuce. Place one shrimp in each leaf. Divide the tarragon among the shrimp. Squeeze the lemon juice across the shrimp. Put a tiny pinch of salt and pepper on each shrimp. Carefully wrap the shrimp to form a compact package. Place in a steamer and set aside.

In the bottom half of the steamer, combine the white wine and clam juice.

In an acid-resistant saucepan, over medium-high heat, reduce the fish fumet and 4 oz. white wine to about ½ cup. In another saucepan, reduce the heavy cream to about ½ cup.

When both are reduced, add the cream to the fumet. Then add the tomato paste and reduce to a light-sauce consistency. Reserve.

When ready to serve, bring the steamer to a simmer, cover and steam the lettuce-wrapped shrimp.

Meanwhile, bring the sauce back to a boil. Add the butter while whisking. Then add the basil, garlic and season to taste. Add the tomatoes.

When the shrimp are just firm to the touch, remove from the heat.

Spoon the sauce onto warm plates. Arrange the shrimp across the plate and sauce. Garnish with French tarragon or basil and serve.   *Serves 4*

BREAST OF DUCK WITH BASIL, HAZELNUTS AND RED WINE

4 breasts of duck, skinned and defatted	2 oz. hazelnuts, skinned and chopped
4 cups duck stock	2 oz. sweet basil, chopped
12 oz. red wine, Côtes du Rhône	1 clove garlic, minced
4 oz. shallots, chopped	1 orange rind, grated
4 baby artichokes, blanched and quartered (or 4 artichoke hearts, blanched and quartered)	4 oz. sweet butter
	salt and black pepper to taste

Reduce the duck stock over medium-high heat to 1 cup. Add the red wine and shallots. Reduce to 1 cup. Reserve.

Slowly sauté the duck breasts in butter to medium-rare. Reserve in a warm place, covered.

Return the sauce to a simmer. Whisk in the butter, tablespoon by tablespoon. Reduce the sauce to medium consistency, when it coats the back of the spoon. Add the artichokes, hazelnuts, basil, garlic and orange rind. Adjust the seasonings.

Spoon the sauce onto the plate. Quickly slice the breast of duck. Fan the breast over the sauce.

Garnish with a sprig of basil and serve.   *Serves 4*

BREAST OF DUCK WITH ARTICHOKES AND PINE NUTS

2 breasts of duck, skinned and defatted
2–2½ cups duck stock
8 oz. red wine, Côtes du Rhône
2 ounces shallots, julienned
4 baby artichoke hearts, blanched, quartered
1 oz. pine nuts, toasted
2 Roma tomatoes, peeled and diced

1 clove garlic, chopped fine
1 bunch basil, chopped fine (or 4–6 sprigs)
salt and black pepper
½ bunch young rosemary, chopped fine (3–4 4-inch sprigs)
8 tbs. sweet butter
fine leaf basil sprig for garnish

Reduce the duck stock over medium-high heat to ½ cup. Add the red wine and reduce to ½ cup.

Lightly sauté the shallots in 2 tablespoons of butter. Add to the reduced stock and wine. Reduce the composite to 2 ounces. Reserve.

Slowly sauté the breasts in 2 tablespoons butter to medium rare. Reserve in a warm place, covered.

Deglaze the pan with a drop of red wine. Add the deglazings to the sauce. Add the garlic, basil, rosemary and the tomatoes to the sauce. Reduce quickly to sauce texture. Add the artichoke hearts and pine nuts. Adjust the seasonings. Quickly stir in 4 tablespoons of butter to finish the sauce.

Spoon the sauce onto the plate. Slice the breast of duck and fan over the sauce. Garnish with a sprig of fine leaf basil and serve. *Serves 2*

MUSSELS AND SCALLOPS À LA CAMARGUE

36 blue mussels
1 lb. bay scallops
2 tbs. shallots, chopped fine
1 clove garlic, chopped fine
4 oz. white wine (Pinot
    Chardonnay)
2 oz. clam juice

2 cups heavy cream
1 tbs. lettuce leaf basil
pinch saffron
8 tbs. sweet butter
salt
white pepper

Mussel Court Bouillon:
handful seaweed
1 bunch parsley (8–10 stems)
1 onion, coarsely chopped
2 cloves garlic, smashed

4 oz. white wine
4 oz. clam juice
12 hot red peppers

Clean the mussels and the scallops. Reserve.

Assemble the court bouillon in a stainless-steel or enameled cast-iron pot. Add the mussels, place over medium heat and cover. When the mussels come to a simmer, shake the pot to distribute the heat every minute or so.

While the mussels are steaming, sauté the garlic and shallots until they are transparent. Increase the heat and add the white wine and clam juice; reduce 50 percent. Add the heavy cream and basil. Reduce to a medium sauce consistency over high heat.

While the sauce is reducing, remove the mussels from their shells. Reserve them.

Sauté the scallops in butter over high heat. Drain off the butter and reserve the scallops.

The sauce should now be reaching the proper consistency.

Add the saffron and adjust the seasonings. When the sauce consistency is reached, add the mussels and scallops. Return to proper sauce consistency and serve.   *Serves 6*

A Fox Hill Farmer's Note:

What's a Sprig? Unraveling an Age-Old Mystery.

A basil sprig is the top three to four leaf clusters on a stem. But most herb sprigs really can't be measured in length because of the differing sizes of herb plants and the varying qualities of their foliage at different times of the year. A sprig of thyme may be less than three inches long, a sprig of rosemary up to 6 inches long, a sprig of parsley just one solitary leaflet.

Fox Hill Farm's Recipes from the Basil Buffet . . .

THE 1982 MENU

Gazpacho with fine leaf basil

Cuke and zuke rounds stuffed with barley pesto

Sweet basil, tomato and cheese sandwiches on party rye

Tabbouleh wrapped in lettuce leaf basil and tied with chives

Fresh veggies with avocado and piccolo verde fino basil dip

Barbecued beef marinated in and stuffed with a basil-mixed herb medley

PESTO GENOVESE

Pickled garbanzos, romanos and onion with nano compatto vero basil*

Mixed greens salad tossed with dark opal basil vinaigrette*

Eggplant salad with sweet and fine leaf basils*

Whole small tomato plugged with bush basil

Watermelon

Iced basil teas

* recipes follow

PICKLED GARBANZOS, ROMANOS AND ONIONS

1 cup dried garbanzo beans
salt
½ lb. Italian green beans
    (romanos)
2 dry mild Spanish or red onions
½–1 cup lemon juice
½ cup fresh Greek oregano
    leaves

2 tbs. fresh rosemary leaves
1 cup fresh nano compatto vero
    basil leaves
a good-sized sprig winter savory
    leaves
¼ cup olive oil
fresh ground black pepper

Place garbanzos in a pot with 3 cups water; heat to a boil, add salt to taste, lower heat and simmer about forty-five minutes until beans are tender but firm. Drain, rinse and set aside.

Remove stem ends from green beans; blanch in boiling water two to three minutes until they start to change color. Drain and rinse in ice cold water. Slice onion into rings. Place prepared vegetables in large container.

Combine remaining ingredients, pour over vegetables and refrigerate three days.

Serve as a side dish. Garnish with fresh inch-long growing point sprigs of nano compatto vero basil.   *Serves 8–10*

When Leonardo painted the Sistine Chapel in Rome, do you suppose he got his inspiration and sustenance from a plate of pesto washed down with a liter of the local red? And have you ever wondered how those great architectural edifices built to honor the deity came to be called BASILicas?

EGGPLANT SALAD

4 lbs. eggplant, any variety
2 lbs. Roma tomatoes, cored and
  quartered
1 large sweet red onion, sliced
  and separated into rings.
2 cups flat leaf parsley (Italian or
  Japanese mitsuba), chopped
1 cup sweet basil, coarsely
  chopped

1 cup French fine leaf basil,
  destemmed
2–3 cloves garlic, minced
1 cup olive oil or salad oil
¼ cup fresh lemon juice without
  the seeds
salt and pepper to taste

Preheat oven to 350 degrees. Pierce skins of eggplants and
place in the oven, middle rack, to bake about thirty-five to
forty-five minutes, until fairly soft but not wrinkled.

Remove eggplants from oven and cool on a wire rack. When
cool, peel and cut into 1-inch chunks.

In a large container with cover, combine all ingredients.
Toss with vigor and purpose. Cover container and refrigerate
overnight.

Garnish with fresh sprigs of basil and parsley.   *Serves 6–8*

MIXED GREENS TOSSED WITH DARK OPAL BASIL VINAIGRETTE

Greens:

1 head buttercrunch lettuce
1 head limestone bibb lettuce
½ head romaine
½ head red leaf lettuce
20 arugola leaves
5 heads mache

10 radicchio leaves or any chicory
20 French sorrel leaves
1 large mild onion, sliced very fine or
6 scallions, sliced very fine

Clean and dry all greens. Shred into comfortable bite-sized pieces and place in a large, chilled salad bowl.

Dressing:

1–2 cups dark opal basil leaves
2–3 cloves garlic
¼ cup fresh lemon juice, seeds removed

1 cup olive oil or vegetable oil
salt and freshly ground pepper to taste
$\frac{1}{16}$ tsp. dry mustard

Process garlic in food processor until finely chopped. Add basil leaves and process until coarsely chopped.

Add lemon juice, salt, pepper and mustard, process quickly.

With processor on, slowly stream in oil until incorporated.

Add dressing to chilled salad greens and toss with vigor. Serve cold.
Serves 6–8

THE 1983 MENU

Tabbouleh on lettuce leaf basil leaves

Greek eggplant salad with nano compatto basil

*Seven fresh raw dipping vegetables
with four dips*

Aioli with dark opal basil

Guacamole with lemon basil

Spinach cheese with bush basil

Remoulade with bush basil

Gazpacho BF83 with piccolo verde fino basil*

*PESTO GENOVESE BF83
with sweet and piccolo verde fino basil*

Mushroom pâté with cinnamon basil*

*Garbanzo, green bean and carrot salad
with fine leaf basil*

Barbecued spareribs with basil paste sauce*

Barbecued chicken with six herbs and sweet basil

Iced lemon balm and mint teas

Watermelon

* recipes follow

Hungry Basil Festival revelers indulged at the Basil Buffet

70 or 80 lbs. of linguini
10 gallons of Pesto sauce
200 slabs of spareribs
710 pieces of chicken
60 gallons of gazpacho
13 bushels of fresh veggies
8 gallons of olive oil
15 lbs. of garlic
countless pounds of 10 varieties of BASIL
4 gallons of Fox Hill Farm herb vinegars
13 pounds of other fresh herbs
what seemed like a ton of ice

And they ate it all up, just about!

CINNAMON BASIL MUSHROOM PÂTÉ

2 lbs. fresh mushrooms
½ cup butter, softened
1 large onion
2–3 celery stalks
8 oz. cream cheese, softened
3 tbs. cream sherry
4 eggs
1½ cups rye bread crumbs

20 peppercorns
8 sprigs each basil, rosemary,
    thyme, sweet marjoram,
    Italian oregano
1 tb. Worcestershire sauce
1 tsp. tabasco sauce
sufficient cinnamon basil
    leaves to line loaf pans

In the bowl of a food processor coarse chop onion and celery. Remove to a large mixing bowl. Coarsely chop mushrooms and add to the mixing bowl. Put bread crumbs in mixing bowl. Toss to incorporate above ingredients.

Grind peppercorns in food processor. Add herb sprigs and coarsely chop. Add eggs and process briefly; add cream cheese and process about thirty seconds. Add butter, process to incorporate. Add Worcestershire, tabasco, sherry and salt to taste.

Mix wet and dry ingredients thoroughly.

Butter two 5 × 9 loaf pans, line with buttered aluminum foil, leaving enough overhang to seal top, and artfully arrange cinnamon or other basil leaves along bottom and sides of pâté pans.

Divide pâté mixture evenly between pâté pans, press in firmly. Top with remaining basil leaves. Seal foil tightly.

Preheat oven to 400 degrees. Place pâté pans in a 3-inch deep water bath. Bake two to three hours. Cool. Chill overnight. Remove foil, slice and serve icy cold.

BASIL GAZPACHO BF83

Soup Base:

2 lbs. Roma tomatoes
1 qt. rich tomato juice
¼ cup rosemary vinegar
2 cloves garlic, peeled
¼ cup Greek oregano vinegar
¼ cup olive oil
2 bay leaves
¼ cup cream sherry
salt to taste

3 sprigs fresh thyme
5 sprigs fresh sweet marjoram
6 sprigs piccolo verde fino
  basil
1 large onion
1 medium cucumber, seeded and
  peeled
1 small zucchini, peeled

Soup Garnishes:

1 lb. Roma tomatoes
1 medium cucumber, in the skin

3 green onions
1 green pepper

Core, quarter and puree the tomatoes, onion, cucumber and zucchini in a food mill, blender or food processor.

Add remaining ingredients, sitr and chill several hours. Float one hot pepper on top to impart a mild tang.

Dice vegetables into bite-sized pieces. Stir into soup. Chill. Serve cold.   *Serves 6–8*

BASIL PASTE BARBECUE SAUCE

1 qt. Open Pit barbecue sauce	1 tsp. paprika
¼ cup Greek oregano vinegar	1 tsp. cayenne
½ cup sweet basil paste (see note)	¼ tsp. tabasco

Combine all ingredients in a 2-quart bottle, shake well, let rest for three days before using.

Lightly coat spareribs with sauce the day before cooking. Refrigerate.

Grill spareribs until just about cooked, then for the last ten minutes of cooking, brush on more sauce, turning ribs frequently to prevent burning.

Throw some basil stems on the fire to enhance the flavor further.

Note: How to make basil paste:

Destem a large quantity of your favorite basil. Quickly pulse-process in food processor to medium-chop. Add just enough olive oil or salad oil to coat lightly. Pack into wide mouth jars to 1½ inches from the top. Float ½ inch oil on top of paste to seal. Store in refrigerator or freezer.

5

Things to Do with Pesto When You're Fresh Out of Pasta

"Verde, que te quiero, verde . . ."

A Spanish poet.
Pablo Neruda, or was it
Federico Garcia Lorca?

Back to the Basics of Pesto

Lest We Forget . . .
Pesto Is Peasant Food

In northern Italy and southern France basils grow like weeds—dependable, reliable and there just waiting for the cook's harvest.

And the other key pesto ingredients—olive oil, Parmesan or other hard grating cheeses (Sardo pecorino, asiago or Romano), garlic—are also basic staples produced from indigenous materials.

Since pesto's roots are in subsistence cooking, every cook makes it a bit differently, depending on what ingredients are on hand and the temper of the palate at the moment. (American potato salad is a similar free-for-all phenomenon.)

On sunny Mediterranean slopes, back in the good old days, before electricity, blenders and food processors, Italian cooks ground their classic mash of basil, garlic, oil and the good, hard grating cheeses of Parma with a mortar and pestle—probably using a bit of salt to make it grate great.

Just a bit to the west, beyond the principality of Monaco, the cooks of Southern France were also pulverizing their basil, but a bit differently. They ground their basil with garlic, then added grilled tomato and oil, and called it pistou. Pistou is used as a seasoning for soups, stews, etc.

Modern cooks, I challenge you to try this authentic pesto-making technique.

First, choose your favorite pesto recipe from among the twelve in Chapter 3. A surprising amount of physical energy is required to produce a smooth paste. You can replace that expended energy by consuming a significant amount of carbo-hydrates. Rx: a large serving of Pesto Genovese—with home-made pasta, of course!

And, when you run out of pasta, here are some ways to use your fine, hand-turned pesto.

The recipes work best when you have some pesto sauce conveniently prepared and safely ensconced in your refrigera-tor. (Just remember to float about an inch of oil on top of the pesto to keep it from discoloring.) None of them should take more than fifteen minutes to prepare.

PESTO-SLATHERED CHICKEN

1 whole 4–5-pound roasting
  chicken or capon
½ cup pesto sauce
salt and pepper to taste

1 clove garlic, peeled
3 sprigs fresh thyme (optional)
1 sprig rosemary (optional)

Preheat oven to 300–325 degrees.

Rinse the bird and pat dry. Remove any remaining pin feathers.

Loosen the poultry's skin by sliding your hands between the flesh and the skin on either side of the breastbone.

Insert the pesto into each pocket and smooth over all the flesh, reserving some pesto—about 4 tablespoons. Glaze the outside of the bird with the reserved pesto, especially the breastbone, thighs and drumsticks.

Salt and pepper the cavity, adding an extra clove of garlic, three sprigs of fresh thyme and one sprig of rosemary, if you like.

Place on a baking rack in a shallow pan in the middle of the oven. Bake uncovered about one hour until the thigh joint is easily manipulated and the bird's juices are clear.

Remove from the oven and let rest for ten minutes before carving.   *Serves 4–6*

PESTO OMELETTE

6 large fresh eggs
2 tbs. water
salt and pepper to taste

¼ cup pesto sauce
2 tbs. butter
2 tbs. olive oil

Preheat a heavy 8-inch frying pan or omelette pan over a high flame. Add 2 tablespoons each of butter and oil, let melt and swirl to coat the cooking surface of the pan.

Separate eggs. Beat egg whites to a soft peak stage, then beat egg yolks until lemon in color. Add salt, pepper and water to yolks and blend. Quickly fold egg whites into yolk mixture.

Pour egg mixture into hot pan, let eggs get firm. With a spatula, gently lift the edge of the firming eggs and allow the unset eggs to drift underneath.

When eggs are just firm, spread the pesto sauce (thinned with a bit of milk or cream if necessary) in a thin strip over the eggs. Fold in the traditional manner and serve hot.   *Serves 2–3*

PESTO-PACKED TOMATOES

4 large round red or yellow
  tomatoes (Big Boy, beefsteak
  and Jubilees are good varieties)

1 cup pesto sauce

Core the tomatoes, but do not skin. Score into 6 to 8 sections, cutting no more than halfway through the tomato.

Allow some of the seeds and freely flowing juice to drain.

Fill the slightly opened tomato cavities with ¼ cup pesto for each tomato.

Oven broil three inches under the flame for five minutes, until tomatoes are hot and pesto is beginning to melt.

Microwave method: Place tomatoes in a shallow round casserole and cover lightly with plastic wrap. Microwave on high for two to three minutes. Let sit five minutes to finish cooking evenly.

Serve hot.   *Serves 4*

PESTO ROULLADE

3 lbs. ground meats—equal parts beef, pork and lamb
1 large onion, coarsely chopped
1 egg, lightly beaten
salt and pepper to taste
¼ cup sherry or dry red wine
1 cup pesto sauce

2 tbs. capers
12 to 15 large black olives, pitted and halved
strips of pimiento, green pepper, Roma tomato or basil rosettes for garnish

In a large mixing bowl combine all ingredients thoroughly except the pesto, capers and olives.

Line a large baking sheet with waxed paper and press the meat mixture into a large rectangle no more than ½ inch thick. Chill to firm up the meat mixture.

Evenly spread the pesto sauce on the meat rectangle and sprinkle with the capers and olive halves.

Lift the waxed paper at the narrow end of the meat and gently, but firmly, roll the meat jellyroll style, lifting and separating the paper from the meat while rolling.

Seal the end of the roll and the sides of the roll by moistening with water and pressing the meat layers together.

Garnish with strips of pimiento or green pepper, thin slices of Roma tomato, and rosettes of fresh basil. Carefully place in a shallow baking pan.

Bake at 325 degrees for about one hour, or until meat thermometer reads 140. Remove from the oven, let rest twenty minutes to firm up before slicing.

Serve hot or cold with basil pepper jelly.   *Serves 6–8*

PESTO-HEARTED PÂTÉ

My son, Charlie, and I used to have a regular ritual. Every day when he came home from school we would make popcorn and watch Julia Child on television. Few things, except visitors to our farm, ever interrupted our Child routine. The following recipe is a modification of a pâté she made on one of those marvelous PBS shows. Writing this recipe would be easier if I could find the hastily written, popcorn-stained original version of so many years ago. We make this regularly; it's especially good served very cold on a hot summer's day.

Talk your butcher into getting you

3 lbs of good fatback. Slice it thin.	3 lbs ground pork with 25% fat content
1 lb. chicken livers marinated in ½ cup cognac or Basil Brandy	2 cups pesto
½ cup cream	24 cashews or Brazil nuts
3 tbs. cognac or Basil Brandy	30–40 basil leaves
3 tbs. thyme	salt and pepper
3 tbs. rosemary vinegar	4 cloves garlic
2 tbs. savory	4 bay leaves
	3 sprigs of thyme

Preheat oven to 350 degrees.

To prepare two 5 × 9 loaf pans, slice fatback into very thin sheets. (It helps to have the fatback very cold and to use a long thin very sharp knife.) Completely line the loaf pans with the fatback slices, allowing enough overhang so that the fatback will be able to cover the pan's contents and overlap a little.

Using a meat grinder or food processor, regrind the ground pork, adding the cream, cognac drained from the chicken livers, destemmed thyme and winter savory, salt and pepper. The texture should be a very fine grind.

Divide the ground and seasoned pork into three parts. Place one part in the fatback-lined pan and smooth it out to make a nice bottom layer. Press with your knuckles to make sure it's packed in the pan with no air bubbles.

Evenly space 12 of the nuts, in rows of three. Top with one half of the livers. Spread 1 cup of pesto on top of the livers.

Add the second third of the ground pork mixture, spreading it evenly on the pesto-topped livers.

Sprinkle on 3 tablespoons cognac. Evenly space 12 more of the nuts in rows of three. Add the rest of the chicken livers. Spread 1 cup pesto on top of livers.

Spread the remaining ground pork mixture and firm into pan.

Top the final layer with 4 bay leaves, 3 sprigs of thyme and sufficient basil leaves to cover the meat surface.

Wrap the top with the fatback overhang, making sure the complete surface of the pâté is fully enclosed in the fatback.

Place pan in a waterbath. Add three inches of hot water to waterbath. Place a heavy ovenproof weight on top of pâté. (We use a foil-covered brick.) Bake about one hour until the pâté's juices run clear.

Remove from the oven. Remove pâté pan with weight from the waterbath. Allow to cool one hour with the weight on. Remove pâté from pan and wrap in aluminum foil.

Refrigerate at least overnight before serving. This improves the flavors and makes slicing easier.

To serve, slice with a thin sharp knife or wire. Serve with cornichons, pickled onions or the like.

Preparation time decreases once you get the hang of slicing the fatback.

PESTO CUCUMBER PINWHEELS

4 long fresh cucumbers
½ lb. alphabet pasta, cooked al
  dente or substitute 1½ cups
  cooked barley

¾ cup pesto
3 tbs. basil vinegar

In a small bowl, mix the cooked pasta, pesto and vinegar and refrigerate to firm.

Scrub any wax from cucumber skin. Score the cucumber lengthwise or peel off alternating strips of peel. Cut off the ends of the cucumbers.

With a long thin knife (use a blade at least half the length of the cucumber), remove the seed cavity of the cucumber and discard. You now have a cucumber tube.

Fill the cucumber tube with the pesto mix, packing the filling in very firmly.

Refrigerate to chill well. Slice thin and serve on a thin mild-flavored cracker like Bremner's plain wafers. Garnish with a small sprig of fine leaf basil or nano compatto vero basil.

Note: You can substitute very young summer squash (zucchini, golden summer squash), mild sweet Italian peppers or Japanese eggplant (the long ones) for the cucumbers. Or get some fresh snow peas, slit them open along their spines and very gently stuff some pesto inside.

EASY PESTO SALAD DRESSING

1 part pesto
2 parts mayonnaise, sour cream
  or yogurt

1 to 2 tbs. marjoram vinegar to
  thin
2 tbs. olive or salad oil

In a small, wide mouthed, sealable container, mix all ingredients, adding vinegar last to thin to desired consistency. Add salt and freshly ground pepper to adjust seasoning.

Refrigerate at least overnight to allow the flavors to marry.

Use on hot vegetables or salads requiring a creamy, thick dressing.

6

Basil Beyond Pesto

It's Okay to Pig Out on Basil.
Here's Help.

If you suffer from that unmentionable malady, known in
some circles as basil-mania, some relief is in sight. A few
menus and recipes follow to showcase, but certainly
not to limit, basil's culinary virtuosity.

These are simply meant to pique your curiosity and send
you scurrying to your ethnic cooking library to identify and
try any number of other basil-luscious recipes that have with-
stood the test of time. Try the cuisines of Italy, France, Spain,
Thailand, the Carribean, India, Iran (modern Babylon), Greece,
Crete and East Africa.

May your explorations be fruitful and your tastebuds titil-
lated.

LET BASIL JOIN YOU AT TABLE FOR DINNER

Caviar on Basilled Sour Cream in Pastry Shells*

Snow Peas Stuffed with Pesto

Basil Champagne

Spring Soup with Basil Flowers*

*Beef Wellington
with Basil Horseradish or Basil Pepper Jelly*

Gratin of Root Vegetables

A voluptuous red wine

Mixed Greens Salad with Dark Opal Basil Vinaigrette

Real Basil Cheescake*

Basil Brandy

* Recipe may be found in this chapter. All other basil recipes appear else-
where in this book.

A SIMPLE BASILLED BREAKFAST

Icy Cinnamon Basil Fruit Compote*

Pesto Omelette

Linda's Toasted Basil Beer Bread*
topped with Basil Butter

Hot Holy Basil Tea*

BASIL BRUNCH OR LUNCH

Cheesy Basil Puffs*

Nao's Peas and Basil Salad*

Pesto-hearted Pâté
and Basilled Cornichons

Pesto Genovese with Piccolo Verde Fino Basil

Artichoke and Crab with Lemon Basil Butter*

Tabbouleh Wrapped in Lettuce Leaf Basil*

Jan's Basil Buns*

Fresh Fruit Tart with Lemon Basil Glaze*

ICY CINNAMON BASIL FRUIT COMPOTE

1 small cantaloupe
1 small honeydew
1 15 oz. can kumquats or lichi
   nuts
1 qt. blackberries
2 crisp firm apples

2 cups simple syrup
1 cup cinnamon basil
6 sprigs sweet woodruff
3 sprigs spearmint
6 large, firm pears

In a small bowl, mix together the basil, sweet woodruff, mint and simple syrup. Refrigerate for twenty-four to forty-eight hours, then remove herbs.

Peel and seed cantaloupe, honeydew and apples. Cut into 1-inch pieces (bite-sized). Drain kumquats or lichi nuts, reserving liquid to add to herbed simple syrup. Destem and clean blackberries.

Combine prepared fruits with herbed syrup. Mix and refrigerate several hours to improve flavors.

Serve in fruit cups made from pears. Remove necks, seeds and all but ½ inch of flesh. Garnish with cinnamon basil flower spike. Preparation time: thirty minutes.   *Serves 6*

LINDA'S BASIL BEER BREAD

Linda Steele is a Fox Hill Farmer. She's in charge of herb produce and vinegar production. Like so many other working folk, her recipes are fast. And, they sure are good.

3 cups self-rising flour
3 tbs. granulated sugar
½ cup sweet basil, chopped

12 oz. warm beer (no specified
   brand)

Mix all of the above ingredients together.

Pour into well-greased standard-sized loaf pan.

Place in an unheated oven. Set oven temperature to 350 degrees, bake fifty minutes.

Remove from pan, cool on wire rack and slice.

HOT HOLY BASIL TEA

4–6 cups of rapidly boiling water   6–8 sprigs of holy basil

Place holy basil and water into a preheated teapot. Cover with a tea cozy and let steep for ten minutes.

Pour into bone china teacups or mugs. Serve plain.

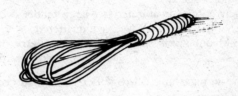

CHEESY BASIL PUFFS

Well-aged, sharp cheddar cheese,   Greek oregano leaves, minced
   grated   Sweet basil leaves, chopped
puff paste

On a floured board, roll out puff paste to $\frac{1}{16}$-inch thickness. Cut into four rectangles.

Lightly dust puff paste rectangle with grated sharp cheddar cheese. Sprinkle with a large pinch of Greek oregano and 3 large pinches chopped basil.

Cover with second rectangle of puff paste. Repeat cheese herb process. Cover with third rectangle of puff paste. Repeat cheese herb process.

Press all layers firmly together.

Cut into 1-inch squares. Keep chilled or freeze.

Preheat oven to 425 degrees. Evenly space squares on cookie sheet, leaving sufficient room between squares for their expansion.

Bake about fifteen minutes, until golden brown and the kitchen is filled with their aroma.

NAO'S PEAS AND BASIL SALAD

Nao Hauser's a farmer's friend and she obligingly shared her favorite basil recipe with us. It's a haunting medley of flavors and textures.

1 small cucumber, seeded and thinly sliced
1 small green pepper, seeded and thinly sliced.
3 green onions, sliced
½ cup finely chopped flat leafed parsley
⅓ cup fresh young peas, shelled
1 small head Boston or bibb lettuce torn in bite-sized pieces
6–8 leaves of Prizehead or other red leaf lettuce torn in bite-size pieces
6 large, tender sweet basil leaves, quartered
3 tbs. raspberry vinegar
½ cup mild olive oil

Mix the vinegar and oil together in a small container. Add salt and pepper to taste.

Gently toss remaining ingredients in a large salad bowl.

Swirl on dressing. And gently toss again.   *Serves 4*

ARTICHOKE AND CRAB WITH LEMON BASIL BUTTER

This is my dear Donald's idea of sustenance for a farmer who's trying to write a book. Soul food.

3 large fresh whole artichokes
¼ lb. lemon basil butter (see Chapter 9)
⅔ lb. fresh crab or lobster meat
1 clove garlic, minced

Trim artichokes and cook in rapidly boiling water until tender. Place upside down in a colander and drain well. Remove the thistle choke and discard.

Place butter and garlic in a small saucepan and heat over a low fire. Keep hot.

Boil crab or lobster until just cooked.

To assemble, gently open artichoke leaves, fill cavity with cooked crabmeat. Pour ⅓ of the hot butter over each artichoke.

Nice with a very crisp light red wine.   *Serves 3*

TABBOULEH WRAPPED IN LETTUCE LEAF BASIL

This ancient Middle-Eastern staple, Fox Hill style, must be good. Over 30 gallons of it were consumed during two Basil Festivals.

4 lbs. finely ground bulghur
14 cups curly parsley, coarsely chopped
12 cups Lebanese mint, coarsely chopped
14 cups sweet onions, chopped
10 cups chives, chopped
50 cloves of garlic, minced
15 cups any old convenient basil, chopped

50 Roma (paste) tomatoes, ripe but firm, chopped
9 cups lemon juice
18 cups fruity olive oil
300 large, prime lettuce leaf basil leaves
300 12–15-inch strands of oriental garlic chives

In a 5-gallon container with a leak-proof lid, add half of the bulghur, parsley, mint, onions, chives, garlic, chopped basil, tomatoes. Mix well, with vigor.

In a blender, emulsify 1 part lemon juice to 2 parts olive oil. Pour over ingredients in 5-gallon container. Mix very well to incorporate.

Add the reserved ½ of the same ingredients and mix well.

In a blender, emulsify more lemon juice and oil. Add to tabbouleh container and mix in well. The mixture should be dressed, but not to excess.

Refrigerate for two days, mixing three times a day. All of the dressing should be absorbed. If the bulghur will take more dressing, add it. Conversely, drain off any excess fluid daily.

To assemble, place 2 tablespoons tabbouleh of each basil leaf near the stem end. Roll and fold in the side edges. Tie lengthwise and widthwise with one strand of oriental garlic chives (regular chives don't work).

Chill.   *Serves 300, more or less!*

JAN'S BASIL BUNS

We used to call Janet "Magic Fingers" because she so quickly mastered the fine art of making cuttings and transplanting delicate, thread-like herb seedlings. Jan is now in charge of all greenhouse operations. She, too, makes bread. This is her recipe, an adaptation of one that appeared in *Prevention* magazine some years ago.

¼ cup lukewarm water	1 tb. rosemary, minced
1 tb. yeast	1 egg
1 tb. honey	½ cup Parmesan cheese, grated
½ cup buttermilk, lukewarm	2–2½ cups whole wheat flour
3 cloves garlic, minced	1 egg beaten with 1 tb. water
3 tbs. sweet basil, minced	(glaze)

Combine water, yeast and honey in a cup. Place in a warm spot until frothy, about ten minutes.

In a large bowl, combine the proofed yeast, buttermilk, garlic, basil, rosemary, and egg. Beat well.

Add cheese and 1 cup of flour, beat well with a wooden spoon. Add enough additional flour to make a soft but kneadable dough—about another cup.

Knead on a lightly floured surface for about five minutes, adding only enough extra flour to prevent sticking. Dough will be slightly tacky, but should be smooth and elastic.

Place dough ball in an oiled bowl, cover and let rise in a warm place until double in bulk, about an hour.

Punch down dough and knead briefly again on a lightly floured surface. Then form into a 12-inch long log. Cut into 12 pieces and form each piece into a smooth ball.

Grease a 9-inch cake pan and place all 12 of the buns in it. Cover, place in a warm spot and let rise again until double in bulk, about thirty to sixty minutes.

Carefully brush the tops of the buns with the egg glaze, being careful not to deflate them. Sprinkle on some extra basil and rosemary if you wish.

Bake at 350 degrees for about twenty-five minutes, until they are golden and sound hollow. Unmold rolls and return to the oven for five minutes to crisp the bottoms.

Serve warm immediately.

FRESH FRUIT TART WITH LEMON BASIL GLAZE

Pastry:

2 cups all-purpose flour	¾ cup butter, cut into chunks
¼ cup sugar	2 egg yolks

In a large bowl, blend flour and sugar. Cut in butter and work into an even texture. Stir in egg yolks. Stir until dough holds together. Shape into a smooth, shiny ball.

Press dough evenly into 12-inch tart pan and bake for about thirty minutes, until golden brown, in a 300-degree oven.

Cool and move pastry from tart pan to serving platter.

Fruit:

Any fruit can be used, but soft pulp fruits are nicest—raspberries, blackberies, blueberries, pears, apple slices, peaches, nectarines, and the ubiquitous kiwi. You'll need 1 to 1½ quarts.

Glaze:

2 cups currant or elderberry juice	1 cup sweet woodruff sprigs, packed
2 cups granulated sugar	1 cup angelica stem pieces
	2 cups lemon basil

Steep basil, woodruff and angelica in juice for three days. Strain and discard herbage.

Put juice and sugar in an enamel saucepan. Cook over medium heat until sugar dissolves and sauce begins to thicken. If not thickening, add more sugar or add 2 tablespoons cornstarch mixed with 5 tablespoons cooled glaze.

Note: If you don't have access to sweet woodruff or angelica, just omit them from the recipe or add a shot of dry vermouth.

To assemble:

Arrange the fruit in the baked pastry shell. Gently pour the glaze over the fruit to cover but don't let it pool in the bottom of the pastry. Let glaze firm up a bit. Slice and serve.

CAVIAR ON BASILLED SOUR CREAM IN PASTRY SHELLS

3 oz. caviar (your favorite brand)
½ cup sour cream
2 tbs. French fine leaf basil leaves

2 tbs. chives, chopped
puff paste shells

Roll puff paste very thin and cut into 2-inch circles. Bake at 450 degrees until just baked, about ten minutes. Cool on wire rack. Cut a well into tops of puffs and remove any soft pastry from inside.

Blend ½ cup sour cream with basil and chives. Let stand several hours for flavors to mingle. Place a tablespoonful of sour cream into hollowed puffs. Garnish with 1½ teaspoons caviar.

SPRING SOUP WITH BASIL FLOWERS

1 quart of a light-flavored, defatted broth like a chicken, veal or fish stock
2 carrots, peeled and jullienned
3 green onions, sliced fine
2 deflowered basil flowering spikes, chopped

⅓ cup chopped chives
⅓ cup fine-cut egg noodles, broken, or bean threads
Flowers from 2 basil flowering spikes

Heat the broth in a saucepan to a simmer, add carrots and cook five minutes. Add onions and chopped basil stems and cook three minutes. Add egg noodles or bean threads and cook five minutes.

Ladle hot into serving bowls and garnish with basil flowers. Serve immediately before the flowers wilt.   *Serves 4*

REAL BASIL CHEESECAKE

I make this cake frequently, and the phone never fails to ring while it's being assembled (that's one of the challenges of working at home), which means that this cheesecake has been successfully made without the sour cream and also without the sugar. Just don't forget the cream cheese or the basil!

2 lbs. cream cheese, room temperature
¾ cup granulated sugar
1 cup sour cream
2 large eggs, lightly beaten
1 cup French fine leaf basil, destemmed

2 tbs. lemon juice (optional)
1 tsp. vanilla
2 tbs. cornstarch
1 cup crushed vanilla wafers or graham crackers
2 tbs. butter

Preheat oven to 450 degrees.

In a food processor or mixer, lightly beat the eggs. Add sour cream, sugar, basil, cornstarch, lemon juice and vanilla. Process until smooth.

Add cream cheese, ½ lb. at a time, and process to incorporate.

Spread softened butter on the bottom and halfway up the sides of a 9- or 10-inch springform pan. Cover buttered area with cookie crumbs, pressing to be sure they stick.

Pour in cheesecake batter and bake for thirty-five to forty-five minutes or until a toothpick inserted in the center comes out clean.

Knife the edges of the cake as soon as cake is removed from the oven. Cool on wire rack about five minutes and remove the side of the pan. Finish cooling, if you can wait.

Cut with dental floss into thin wedges.   *Serves 10*

7

Old Mother Hampstead's Horticultural Hints:

How to Grow Prodigious and Copious Quantities of Basil Anytime and Anywhere

First, Be Sure You've Got Basil Seed . . .

Tiny, dark brown, almost black seeds nestle in the safety of the withered basil flowers until a brisk shake releases them into a hospitable hand. Thus, basil's unending life cycle begins again.

To identify basil seed, grab your calipers and enlist the power of your nose.

Basil seed is ovoid in shape, 1.2 to 1.9 mm wide and 1.4 to 2.9 mm long. Even in the seed stage, there is the sharp fragrance of the plant to come.

Sweet basil seed, and the other *Ocimum basilicum* cultivars, have characteristic sweetened clove scents. The lemon basil seed smells even more citrus-like in the seed stage, and the sacred, holy basil's seed carries a hauntingly sweet, heady perfume distinctive only to it.

Some species' seeds have a whitish nub at the point where the seed was attached to the calyx, or the seed pod. And lemon basil seed shows a distinct gray-black color atypical of the rest of the genus.

Ocimum basilicum seed produces a mucilaginous coating when the seed is moistened. But the sacred, holy basils (Tulsi) seed are non-mucilaginous.

Fox Hill Farmer's Note:

Some varieties of basil seed have a mucilaginous capsule that develops when the seed is moistened. People in some Central American countries and the Caroline Islands take advantage of this mucilage and use the moistened basil seed to remove debris from the eye. Foreign particles in the eye stick to the gel surrounding the basil seed, thus making them easy to remove. You, however, should not attempt this use of basil seed. Grow it and eat it instead!

Plant It Indoors

Sweet basil may well be the original sun worshiper; it exhibits its best personality in the heat of midsummer.

Let that be a significant clue to sowing the seed. Basil seed germinates best in soil temperatures between 75 and 85 degrees Fahrenheit. Some germination will occur at lower temperatures, but the percentage of the seed that will germinate will significantly drop.

So, sow the basil seed varieties of your choice in a sterile, moist growing medium about four to six weeks before the last frost-free day in your area. Here on the farm we use a mix of equal parts of fine-grade vermiculite and perlite that has been well moistened.

Sow the seed fairly thinly as the basils usually germinate well. Cover the seed to twice their size, a scant 1/8 inch, then press gently but firmly to insure good, close contact with the moistened growing medium. Since the growing medium was good and moist when the seeds were sown, there is no need to water after covering the seed. Label the container with the variety name and the date of sowing.

Now, cover the sowed container with clear plastic. The plastic cover will keep the moisture from evaporating; if the seeds dry out before they germinate, they will lose a lot of their germinating potential and your seedling crop size will be diminished.

Place the covered seed container in a nice, warm spot. On top of a radiator, on top of the refrigerator or near another heat source are some options. But don't "cook" your basil seed-bed. Check the seed container every day for signs of germination. Under optimal conditions, most varieties of basil will begin to germinate within three days.

Once the green rash appears on top of the growing medium (that indicates that germination is beginning), loosen, but do not remove, the plastic cover. The cover should be loose enough to provide some ventilation to the emerging seedlings. Good ventilation is important to prevent damp-off, a deadly fungus disease to which many a seedling succumb.

Remove the clear plastic covers a couple of days after germination seems to be completed and the seedling leaves are fully open. You need to orchestrate a simple harmony of the elements to support the vulnerable seedlings during their first week of active growth. The young succulent seedlings need all the light they can get. Light and warmth are as important nourishment to the seedlings as are dilute fertilizers and moisture.

Once the first set of true leaves emerge, about seven days after germination, it is time to transplant the delicate basil seedlings. Again, provide a sterile growing medium for transplanting such as a peat lite mix or sterilized potting soil.

Transplant the seedlings into individual two-inch pots to grow on for another month. Or transplant them into a community flat at least two inches deep, spacing the seedlings two inches apart in rows three inches apart. At this point, the seedlings are only one week of age and very tiny. The temptation will be to plant them too closely together. Resist that temptation. Remember the ultimate size of the basil bushes!

(Quickly review Personality Profiles and remember that sweet and piccolo verde fino basils will grow to over two feet high and about two feet wide in a scant eight weeks once transplanted into their final garden plot.)

Give your young transplants lots of light; a sunny windowsill on the south or west side of your house will have the best light.

Then, to the garden they go!

About 3000 B.C., just after the dawn of civilization, in the great Mesopotamian fertile plains, basil grew bountifully, sustained by the Tigris River.

". . . Many herbs were brought under cultivation and featured prominently in the early Assyrian and Babylonian gardens which grew amongst others cumin, sesame, mint, *basil,* coriander, anise, thyme, asafoetida, bay, fennel, rocket (arugola), saffron and sage. Many others were known, like mustard seed and capers, as well as the ubiquitous and highly popular leeks, onions, garlic and chives."

Food in Antiquity, Don and Patricia Brothwell, Frederick A. Praeger, New York, 1969. (Emphasis added.)

Sow the Seed Outdoors

Most of the many varieties of basil are easy to grow from seed directly sown in the soil out of doors. Just learn and respect basil's simple growing rules and you won't go wrong. Bending the rules too far, however, will lead to a basil misadventure.

So, first things first.

Soil

The garden's soil is a complex mixture of organic and inorganic substances, interspersed with air and water. Take a soil test to determine what your garden plot offers. (The local County Co-operative Extension Service offers soil testing for individuals at a nominal cost.)

Basil requries a pH range of 6.4 to 7.0 to best use the nutrients in the soil. Strive for an organic matter content in your soil of more than 3 percent. Major soil nutrient levels are the same as required to grow corn and tomatoes, i.e. a higher level of N (nitrogen) in proportion to P (phosphorus) and K (potassium). The trace elements (micro nutrients) should be in balance, too. Structurally, the soil should have good to excellent air and water exchange capacity. If your garden will grow tomatoes or corn, it will grow basil.

Armed with that information, correct the soil by adding and tilling in the substances recommended—peat moss, compost to improve soil structure, fertilizers, lime to correct nutrient levels. Incorporate these materials into the top eight inches of the soil.

Yes, it is a lot of hard work but you need to create an inviting, supportive environment. And, basil will let you know if it considers its environment hostile!

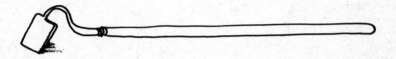

Heat

Optimum range: 50–100 degrees Fahrenheit.

Basils grow best with warm soil and warm, humid air. Cold soils cause basils to languish or rot. Cold air causes leaf discoloration in the form of nasty blackened spots. When the soil in your garden warms up to at least 50 degrees, and all danger of frost has past, it's then safe to transplant your baby basils.

Light

10,000 foot candles and more!

The same sun that provides the heat for basil also provides its light, and basil demands lots of it. So make sure the basil patch is located where it will get at least six hours of full sun each day. However, in hot harsh arid regions like deserts, provide some shade for basils in the afternoon—just let it bask in the gentle morning sun.

Moisture

Rain is the best moisture but Mother Nature does not parcel out that precious fluid in measured, regular amounts. So you need to intervene and provide water. Like corn and tomatoes, basil likes a soil that holds water, but yet is well drained. For heavy loam and clay soils, provide at least an inch of water a week. For lighter loam and sandy soils, water twice as frequently, 1 inch twice a week, and mulch the root zones to preserve that moisture and to keep the soil moisture at an even level. Don't let the soil get dry to the point of wilting and then waterlog it to compensate.

Fertilization

Basil is crazy about the big "N," nitrogen, which makes the leaves a deep rich green. But nitrogen must be in balance with all the other nutrients. Usually, with good soil testing and preparation before planting, additional fertilization is not necessary.

But sometimes during the height of the harvest season, a dose of plant food is helpful. Watch how your basil is responding to repeated cuttings in July and August. If regrowth starts to slow down, you respond with some grow power; fish emulsion, compost or a tomato-formulated chemical fertilizer are good choices. (Fresh manure or incompletely composted manure can cause trouble—either burn your basil or sprout a fine, rich crop of weeds!)

Insect pests

In the natural environment, basils have few pests. An occasional leaf hopper larva or spittle bug may find sustenance in its leaves. White flies from nearby tomatoes or verbena may stop, but not stay. No human intervention is required unless extensive damage starts to appear. Choose your chemical weapons carefully, if you must use them.

Basil's biggest threat comes when it's most vulnerable, the first two weeks or so after transplanting. If your garden has cutworm problems, then protect your young plants with cutworm stopping collars on transplanting. Cutworms, however, do not like lime and woodashes. Sprinkle either of these in a four-inch circle on the soil around the base of the plant, taking care not to touch the basil's stem. But if the soil pH is high enough, cutworms should not be a problem.

Maintaining your basils outdoors

If you are eating your bountiful basil regularly, you will automatically be doing the major part of basil maintenance—pruning. To keep basil plants well groomed and producing tasty, tender leaves at optimum levels, regular pruning is a must. Unless your goal is to produce seed, cut off the flowering spikes before they get much longer than an inch or two in length. Flavor changes begin to take place in the leaves when the flowering spikes are allowed to develop. Cut off the flowering spike just below the large leaf cluster beneath it. It's that simple.

The only other regular maintenance that basil requires is basic soil cultivation to keep the soil texture loose and weeds to a minimum. That's all there is to it.

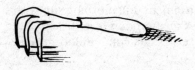

To Pot or Not

'Tis the major dilemma of the serious basil devotee. The answer lies solely with the environment and nurturing you can provide.

Growing medium

Use a sterile, preferably peat-lite, growing medium. Add perlite and/or vermiculite to lighten the texture of the growing medium so that it is open and loose, or just choose a cactus and succulent growing mix blend. Incorporate a well-balanced, time-release fertilizer into the growing mix, but *do not use a systemic insecticide* if you want to use the container-grown plants for food purposes.

Garden soil is not a good option for container-grown plants because it can harbor soil-borne diseases and insects which are kept in balance outside, but can be deadly in a restricted environment like a pot.

The pot

The pots for your basils should be large enough in size to easily accommodate the root system with some room for root growth. Do not crowd the root ball, but a too large container is not wise either. Select container size as you would a pair of shoes for a growing child, a bit big.

It matters not whether your containers are glazed or unglazed terra-cotta, plastic, glass, cardboard or untreated wood. What does matter, however, is that the container have several drainage holes in its bottom to minimize the opportunity for overwatering and the root rot that can result.

Light

Light is the key to successful container-grown basil. In an outdoor environment, full morning sun with some high shade in the heat in the afternoon is in order.

Once the basil plants come indoors, however, all the rules change.

Basil needs very strong light from a south-facing window to be successful as a windowsill plant. As day length and light intensity decrease, basil responds by losing its vibrant color and firmness of tissue. Growth becomes slower and straggly. To keep the plant shapely, just prune it regularly, and of course eat the prunings!

In early February, windowsill basils will begin to announce the coming of spring. The color will improve, and new buds will begin to emerge from the hard, woody stems. That's basil's response to more and better quality light.

An artificial light garden is ideal for growing basil indoors and better on a year-round schedule. Cool white and warm white fluorescent bulbs used in a one-to-one combination produce good growth. Since you do not want to promote flowering, the specially formulated fluorescent tubes are not necessary.

The trick to using artificial light for growing any crop is to make sure you are providing sufficient light intensity and day length. Remember, basil is a sun lover.

Light intensity is a function of the distance of the tops of the basil from the light tubes. The closer the better. You can achieve optimum light intensity, without burning, when the lights are about four inches above the tops of the plants.

So, plug those fluorescent lights into a timer and let them operate fourteen to sixteen hours per day. Or, try capturing the stored effect of light on the plant's tissues by burning the lights for 6 hours, then off for two hours, on for another six hours, then off for the balance of the twenty-four–hour cycle. This saves electrical energy.

Fox Hill Farmer's Note:

The secret of successful basil pot culture.

Good roots do matter. And, given the restrictions of container-growing a shrub, taking care of the roots will go a long way to assuring healthy, viable top growth.

Moisture

Basil ain't no fish nor camel.

In other words, pay attention to watering. Container-grown plants shouldn't be watered on a strict schedule, but rather, as is needed. Porous containers lose moisture more quickly than non-porous pots. Loose growing mixes dry out faster than heavier sterilized potting soil. And, when basil gets strong light from any source—natural or artificial—it will require more frequent watering than during the short light days of dull mid-winter skies.

Learn to read the moisture needs of your potted basils by looking at the leaf changes. Be sure to water before they wilt to keep them growing without a setback.

Another good rule of thumb is to check the bottom of the root ball. Water when the top inch or so of growing medium is dry and the bottom is just damp. Water thoroughly. Don't water again until the growing medium dries out.

Remember, most container-grown plants thrive on benign neglect and basil is no exception.

Fertilizer

Choices. There are several, and it depends . . .

Again, basil is a fairly heavy feeder. The trick in container-growing basil is to match the fertilizing type and schedule to the growing conditions. Fertilize more frequently when basil is in its fast-growth mode. Decrease fertilization when growth slows, otherwise you will stimulate weak growth to the detriment of the entire plant.

Fish emulsion, a well-balanced house plant fertilizer and time-release fertilizer are all acceptable diets for container-grown basil.

The choice is yours. You can choose to feed with every watering if you use fish emulsion or houseplant fertilizer; just use it at one half the strength recommended on the label. Or fertilize monthly at full strength. Time-release fertilizers vary from brand to brand. Follow the label directions.

Have you tickled basil's roots lately?

Make it a point to slip basil out of its container and check its root system regularly (once every four to six weeks or so). Is it pot-bound? Is root rot setting in? Both of these conditions will significantly decrease your yields from container-grown basils. Learn to read the roots. Nice fat white roots are active roots eagerly lapping up the nutrients available and growing at the optimum rate determined by other environmental factors.

Black roots can mean root rot, primarily caused by overwatering. Repot immediately, removing the black roots and *cutting off at least half of the green growth.* After such radical surgery, basil will be in shock, so *do not fertilize or expose to extremely bright light or heat* for about ten days. Repot in a container that is just barely large enough to contain the root system. New hair roots need to grow again to reestablish basil's viability. Basil's death may well be imminent, so be prepared for this harsh lesson.

On the other hand, a mass of tangled dark roots coiled around and around means you have not been monitoring the roots and basil is pot-bound. Remove 20 percent of the roots and growing medium to stimulate new root growth and then replant in a container the same size or one container-size larger. Place the newly repotted basil in a sheltered spot for a few days as it recovers from transplant shock.

Now that you have Old Mother Hampstead's basil-growing secrets, you're ready to grow!

8

Basil in the Plot:

Three Gardens

Sage gardener's advice:
green side up!

Question.
What do you do when every single basil seed germinates?
Answer.
You unmask your secret passion for basil and . . .

. . . Amaze your friends with your gardening skill.

. . . Titillate your neighbors with your *nouveau* landscaping concepts.

. . . And once word of your gardening escapades spreads, you'll be surprised at how many new friends you will make just for a fistful of basil. (The Pied Piper never had it so good.)

Three basil gardens are about to spread before you. Pick one, combine them or simply let them be the inspiration for your own gardening imagination.

Amaze Your Friends with the Amazing Basil Maze

This classic maze is the ideal replacement for a poor grass or sod lawn in a suburban or urban yard. Just think, no more mowing!

Labyrinths and secret spaces have intrigued people since the earliest times. This garden is a modern manifestation of an old idea, and instead of being interpreted in stone, metal, boxwood or yew, you can do it with basil.

The central area is especially designed to be large enough to accommodate a table, some chairs and a brazier—a spot for refreshment for those traipsing merrily through your maze. Another garden seat is strategically placed for the faint at heart.

Rest assured no one will ever get lost in your Amazing Basil Maze; the bushes won't grow much more than 2½ feet tall. However, the Amazing Basil Maze will pose new challenges when entered solely by the light of the silvery moon.

First, locate your plot's spot

The sun should shine upon the spot for the maze at least eight hours a day. The site should be well drained and fairly level. Keep it away from the heavy shadows of buildings and trees, lest the growth be uneven.

At stake is the center

Place a stake in what will be the center of the maze. Use twine or string and four additional stakes to dissect the area into quarters. Make the distance twenty feet from the center stake to the outer edge where you will place one of the four perimeter stakes.

Now find the corners

Tie two ten-foot lengths of twine to each of the four perimeter stakes. Stretch each length in opposite directions and lay them on the ground. Pull the left-hand twine of one stake and the right-hand twine of the adjoining stake to make a right angle (90 degrees) and plant a corner stake. Do the same to find the other three corners. You now have a forty-foot square with three stakes marking each side and a ninth marking the middle.

How to Construct
the Amazing Basil Maze

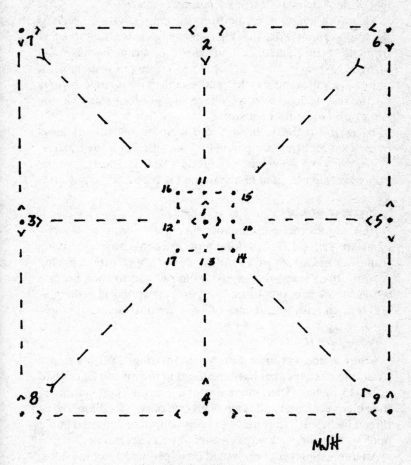

MJH

Requirements:

264 sweet basil plants
1,600 to 2,000 square feet of land
2 balls of twine or string
15 to 20 stakes

Establish the walkways and the respite area

Look carefully at the schematic drawing of the maze and you will see that the basil hedgerows and walkways are each two feet wide. The respite area is eight feet square.

Tie a foot-length of twine from the center stake to each of the four corner stakes, making four triangles. Measure five feet from the center stake on line with the perimeter stake and plant a stake at each of four places. Tie two-foot lengths of twine to each of these stakes and establish right-angle corners for the respite area. Now you have an eight-foot square in the center of a forty-foot square.

To establish the walkways and planting beds, mark lines every two feet that are parallel to the sides of your squares. Then, using the schematic as a guide, mark the location of the walkways. Simple. (If at first you don't succeed, try, try again.)

Pave a maze

Next comes the decision about paving for your walkways. First, forget sod. For a long-term garden consider paving stones or bricks set in a sand base. For shorter-term paving (two to three years) that is easy to install and to walk on, use whole, thick sections of newspaper overlapped like shingles and topped with four inches of aged sawdust or wood chips.

Now plant

Begin at the entrance into your Amazing Basil Maze and plant one or two sweet basil seedlings in the middle of the bed every 15 inches. Then move into the interior beds, starting at the end of each bed and again plant one or two seedlings every fifteen inches. It's important to keep your basil centered in the beds so that the walkways are straight and accessible.

An interesting variation would be to plant some of the beds, selectively, with piccolo verde fino basil, licorice basil and French fine leaf basil. Then perhaps enclose the respite square in the beautiful bi-color Genovese basil. These varieties grow to about the same height as sweet basil.

Maintain a maze

For the first month to six weeks after planting, due vigilance must be kept to root out any and all unbecoming weeds in the basil beds. Of course, there is a simpler way—simply lay black plastic mulch on the basil beds prior to planting. Then cut small holes to insert and plant the young plants.

Once your basil hedges are established, the next maintenance chore will be to keep them in shape by harvesting regularly enough to minimize flowering. For when the basil begins to flower, its form begins to fade.

If worse comes to worst and you can't eat the basil fast enough to keep the flowering at bay, it's quite all right to take out your trusty sharp hedge pruners and give your Amazing Basil Maze a good once-over. You can cut back its height about halfway without jeopardizing its well-being. And rest assured the rough edges will fill out with new, lusciously succulent rosettes within a week or so.

At summer's end . . .

Let the faint smell of frost be the signal for a lingering stroll through your Amazing Basil Maze. For at any time that chilly finger of autumn can fall upon the magic of the maze, turning shining green to speckled black then instant death, leaving behind the skeletal remains as a reminder of the transitory cycle of the season.

Tie One On

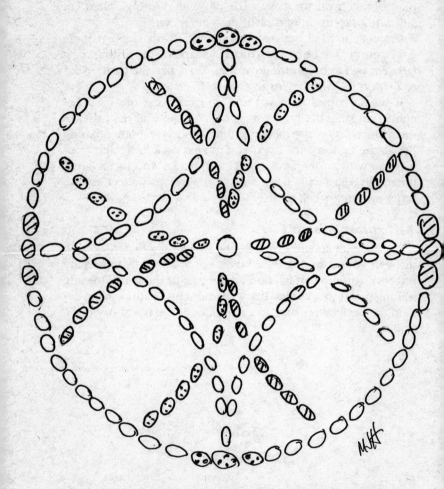

This basic medallion knot garden set in an expanse of lawn will gleam like a jewel. And, you will go down in history for creating edible art!

A twelve-foot circle features three basils

The charm of the Basil Knot Garden comes from planting patterns of three varieties of basil that will grow out to look like they are woven into the warp of your yard. Select varieties of basil of similar size and with contrasting foliage texture and color.

Three Knot Garden variations are provided to get you started. The third option features perennial herbs rather than basil.

Requirements:

94 basil plants (50 for Area 1, 22 for Area 2, 22 for Area 3)
144 square feet of land
10 stakes

To establish the circular Knot Garden

First, find a good sunny location. Then set a center stake and scribe a thirteen-foot circle. Remove all sod from the circle, and till the soil deeply and with vigor several times on succeeding days.

Then scribe a twelve-foot circle and mark it into quarters, then eighths. Finally, scribe semicircles to every other eighth point. The scribe marks will overlap.

Now, plant the basils

Follow the Knot Garden diagram carefully to determine which basil variety to plant in a given area. Plant the same variety in those areas marked 1, switch to another variety for the areas marked 2 and plant the third variety in the areas marked 3. Strict attention to detail will help in your final result.

3 Planting Options for the Circular Knot Garden.

	Garden 1	Garden 2	Garden 3
Area 1	dark opal basil	piccolo verde fino basil	germander
Area 2	lemon basil	Genovese basil	santolina incana
Area 3	nano compatto vero basil	sweet basil	santolina virens

A Simple Salad Border Boasts Basils

Here's Quick Relief from the Long, Dull, Garden Row Syndrome

Nowhere is it written that gardens must be laid out in long straight rows. That concept is a carry-over from fields which must have long straight rows to accommodate mechanical cultivation equipment.

In the smaller plot, you can use your salad and vegetable plants to paint a pretty, eye-catching montage—so much more interesting to look at, yet just as yielding in terms of the garden's production.

Flank a sidewalk with this quick and easy border garden. Or, for a different foundation planting, choose the southern or western exposures of a building for its location. Remember, basil needs lots of sun.

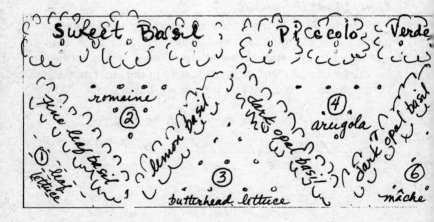

In the Simple Salad Border, the tall robust basils form a backdrop for the zigzag staccato and textural patterns of the lettuces and more diminutive basils.

How to Plot the Salad Border's Zigzag Design

This salad border can be any length you want it to be. Stake out the length in increments of five to six feet, then plot a five- to six-foot width. Establish the back border first by making a parallel line two feet in from the back. This long narrow bed is where your tall basils will go.

Now plot out the zigzags starting at the front of the border, placing the first stake four feet from the corner. The following stakes are spaced every six feet, with the last stake again four feet from the other corner.

To locate the back points of the zigzag, place the first stake seven feet from the narrow edge along the inner parallel line. Place the next stakes every six feet, with the last stake ending at seven feet from the other edge. Now tie off the salad border with twine or string to establish the planting pattern.

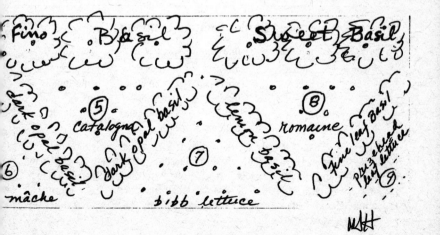

Understand Mother Nature to Maximize Your Salad Border Harvests

You can start planting part of this garden a full month before the last frost-free date in your area. Carefully lay out the garden's design first.

After you've laid out the garden's design, carefully spot where your salad greens will go in each triangle. Make sure you leave six inches on either side of the twine clear for footpaths. Then plant the various greens, one variety per triangle. Use either one plant per spot or two to three seeds per spot, spacing them six inches apart in rows. Salad greens have some degree of frost tolerance and achieve their best flavors when grown in the cool days of early spring and fall.

Once the weather warms the soil, then plant your basils—back border and zigzags. By this time, the salad greens will be thriving and ready for early salads; harvest leaf by leaf at this time to maintain the garden's design.

By midsummer, the basils will be lush but the salad greens will begin to look ragged. Restoration is in order. Remove all the plants from one triangle, spade the soil thoroughly, rake smooth and immediately replant with the same salad green. Replace only two or three beds a week so your garden does not look naked in midsummer.

Salad Border Planting Continuum

early April	mid May	mid June	early July	late August
all greens	all basils	greens: prizehead mache bibb buttercrunch	greens: romaine arugola catalogna	all greens or substitute spinach and red chicory

What's in a name? Mache can be called feticus or lamb's lettuce or corn salad, but whatever the name, these mild-tasting green rosettes are four to six inches in diameter. Arugola is also know as rucola and salad rocket. Its long leaves taste of a hint of sesame. Catalogna can be leaf chicory, cichoria or radichetta. All add interesting, different tastes and textures to the mixed salad bowl.

9
Preserving Basil

Siempre Ocimum

Fresh Really Is Best, But . . .

Like life, being hooked on fresh basil means compromises.

Among those compromises is laying in a basil larder to assure an adequate supply for use when Mother Nature won't provide.

We can get fancy and call it our *tour d'un autre temps.*

Or, we can simply rationalize our squirrel-like behavior by telling friends we're just doing our share as members of the secret Save The Basil Foundation. And, every so often, invoke the secret passwords, "Mr. Green."

Whatever—the bottom line is to assure a substantial basil flow on an annualized basis.

How, When and Where to Harvest Basil

A Snip in Time, Keeps It Fine

Basil is a bountiful producer when it's well nurtured. Keeping it productive and taking volume harvests from a single planting in a growing season is not all that difficult.

The secret's simple.

KEEP BASIL FROM BLOOMING BY REGULAR PRUNING.

And, of course, the prunings are part of your harvests. From about four to six weeks after transplanting or six to eight weeks after sowing seed, basil is ready to yield its first bounty.

Basil in the New World

It seems Thomas Jefferson had an unmet need for basil! His friend George Divers just couldn't provide . . .

> "I am sorry I cannot supply you with all the pot-herbs wanted, we have not the sweet marjoram, sweet basil, or summer savory. I send you some marjoram, winter savory and thyme."

And, a quick look at the Mount Vernon kitchen garden planting list reveals that bed no. 32 held copious quantities of sweet basil, bordered by rue. Could George Washington, too, have had a yen for pesto?

But, why didn't George share his sweet basil with Tom?

Thomas Jefferson's The Garden Book, annotated by Edwin Betts, American Philosophical Society, 1944, reprinted 1974.

A Fox Hill Farmer's Note:

Caution: Don't Bruise the Basil!

Use large, loose containers to hold the basil harvest. Basil bruises very easily and that bruising quickly oxidizes, resulting in somewhat blackened basil. Blackened basil is still good to eat, but loses some of its eye appeal. To quote an ancient oracle: "To be forewarned, is to be forearmed."

The Pick of the Crop

The choicest part of the basil plant is the top, voluptuous leaf cluster—four leaves—the growing point, the flowering point.

Removing this leaf cluster when basil is only six- to eight-leaf clusters tall will cause it to branch faster. The ends of each resulting branch will then produce another prime leaf cluster.

The Maxi Crop

After that initial pruning and the resulting branching, substantially larger harvests can be taken to provide volume for processing. Cut back the basil to about four leaf nodes from the ground. Yes, the plants will look barren, but given the conditions of midsummer, in about three weeks or so, they will have regenerated their glory.

This heavy pruning technique can be used two to three times a season, if the initial cut is early enough in the growing season. Remember, by mid-September, basil's flavor quality begins to diminish as the day length shortens and light intensity drops.

Take Basil to the Laundry

Should, perchance, the basil harvest require washing, use copious amounts of lukewarm water with a drop or two of detergent or water softener to break the water's surface tension.

For large harvests, the bathtub or laundry tub provides lots of room. Again, washing too much at one time can cause basil bruising—a dreaded happenstance in the ideal household.

Quickly swish or plunge the basil in the water to loosen and float off any dust particles. Basil's flavor will go down the drain if it is left to soak in the water for an extended period of time as some of its essential oils are water soluble.

When's Prime Time?

The very best time for harvesting basil, or any other herb, for that matter, is after the morning dew has dried and before the heat of the day. Basil's essential oils are heat activated, and those marvelous fragrances wafting in the air at noontime mean the diminishment of that day's total supply of oil. But if an after-dew harvest is not practical, never fear. Fortunately, basil's copious amount of essential oils means that losing some by off–prime-time harvesting is not going to make a significant difference in the quality of the resulting product.

Now that you've got it, do something!

Pick Your Preserving Method— It's like money in the bank!

Liquid Extractions
  vinegars
  oils
  potable alcohols
  non-potable alcohols
  non-alcoholic potables
  water
  jellies

Pastes
  in oil
  in sweet butter
  in frozen water

Whole Leaves
  drying
  salting
  freezing
  oiling

Seeds

Flowers

Liquid Extractions

The essential oils of basil can be captured in a number of different liquids. This is especially convenient when flavor, but not herbage, is desired.

How to Make Basil-Flavored Vinegars

Loosely pack any variety of basil, stems and all, into a large (gallon-size is nice) wide-mouthed container. Fill the container about three quarters full to within an inch of its top with your favorite, most frequently used, vinegar. (Our choice is 5 percent white distilled vinegar because it has no characteristic flavor of its own that could mask the basil's flavors.)

Press down the herbage that floats upward so that it is submerged in the fluid. Seal the container with a non-metallic lid. This is important as the acids in vinegar can cause metal lids to corrode.

Shake the container and open it to release air bubbles. Store for about four weeks in a cool, dark place (the wine cellar is a good choice). Shake the containers and release air occasionally.

Decant into smaller containers, adding a fresh basil sprig as a built-in label.

Do not store in bright light or on a sunny windowsill as the light will bleach out the delicate herbal colors.

For variety, you can make combination vinegars. Try basil, oregano, one small hot pepper and four cloves of garlic. Another combination could be basil, French tarragon and thyme.

Dark opal basil makes the most beautiful of all the herb vinegars—a glowing, jewel-like purple. Sweet basil, lemon basil, holy basil and the others produce a green-toned color. The flavors are excellent and each has its own characteristic flavor.

CREAMY BASIL HORSERADISH SAUCE

This recipe is dedicated to my father, Matthew Zapalski, whose fine values and traditions I cherish and who has cried regularly every week before Easter since I can remember as he makes fresh horseradish, Polish-style, to accompany his excellent homemade and smoked kielbasa. And that's the root of the matter.

1 cup horseradish, freshly dug and grated	½ cup sour cream
½ cup basil vinegar (not dark opal)	1 cup sweet cream, lightly whipped
½ cup sweet basil, coarse chopped	salt to taste (optional)

If you are using a hand grater to grate the peeled horseradish root, do it outside in the breeze to minimize eye irritation. Otherwise, cut the root into cubes, run them through the food processor or food mill and quickly submerge in the vinegar.

Combine ingredients and place in a tightly sealed container. Refrigerate overnight and serve cold with full-bodied foods.

How to Make Basil-Flavored Oils

The technique for making basil-flavored oils is almost identical to making the vinegars.

Again, start with a large, wide-mouthed container. Remove the leaves, soft stems and flowers from the stems and place them loosely in the jar. Reserve the stems, fastening the ends with a rubber band.

Fill the jar to ¼ inch of the rim with your most frequently used salad oil—mild or fruity olive, corn, safflower or whatever.

Carefully knife out any and all air bubbles. Seal the container and shake vigorously to make any remaining air bubbles rise to the top. Take off the lid to expel the air. Recap and place in a warm, but not hot, place for a week. Shake the container and release air bubbles daily.

After two weeks, strain and discard the basil. Taste the oil to see if its flavor is pronounced. If it is not, strain out the basil and add a fresh batch of basil leaves, soft stems and flowers, being careful to expel the air. Wait another two weeks and strain again, discarding the herbage.

Rebottle in convenient sized narrow-necked bottles and store in a cool dark place. You don't want your fine quality basil oil to get rancid!

Try using French fine leaf, piccolo verde fino, sweet or cinnamon basils. If you regularly use a lot of garlic, drop a couple of cloves in too.

Potable Alcohols

And what do you suppose gives each different brand of vermouth its distinctive taste? Each is flavored with its own special blend of herbs, including basil.

The roots of many of the potable, flavored alcohols are in medicine. The restorative, healing properties of herbs were captured and preserved in potable alcohols—cough medicine.

You can make your own home brew, in the tradition of the greatest cellarmasters of all times, the Benedictine monks of the mountains of southern France.

Choose the base alcohols carefully, as making your own potables can get expensive rather quickly. Select brands of the quality that you would normally buy, or one grade better. Using lesser quality will yield lesser quality.

> Champagne or sparkling wines with
>   carbonation released
> light- to medium-bodied red wines
> white wines
> cognac
> brandy
> vodka
> gin (already flavored with juniper berries)
> (You can also try bourbon, scotch and rye, but
> their flavors are so pronounced that they may
> not be as suitable.)

The method is the same as for making vinegars and oils.

Fill a quart or half-gallon wide-mouthed container with basil—French fine leaf, thrysiflora, lemon and dark opal basils are good choices, as is sweet basil. Add your choice of potable alcohol to ½ inch from the container's rim. Press down herbage. Seal, shake and release air bubbles.

Store in a cool dark place for two to three weeks. Taste. If the flavor is not strongly pronounced, strain out the herbage and replace with fresh herbs. Do this quickly to minimize exposure to air.

Again, seal, shake, release air bubbles and store for two to three months or so. Taste. Strain and decant into smaller containers. Seal securely and label.

BASIL CHAMPAGNE

1 oz. Basil champagne
  concentrate (made using
  the above directions)
3 oz. champagne or sparkling
  wine

French fine leaf basil sprigs for
  garnish
1 Alpine strawberry or 1
  raspberry for garnish

Into chilled, fluted champagne glasses add the berry, basil champagne concentrate and then the sparkling wine.

Do not stir. Garnish with tiny basil sprig or floret. Serve very cold, about 45 degrees Fahrenheit.

BASIL BRANDY

3 large handfuls of lemon basil
  leaves, soft stems and flowers,
  or another type of basil
1 handful of sweet woodruff
1 angelica leaf

6 sprigs French tarragon
½ handful Roman wormwood
  (Artemisia ponticum)
1 fifth brandy

Twist and cram all of the herbs into a quart canning jar. Pour in the brandy. Stir to release air bubbles. Seal, shake, expel air bubbles. Seal and store in a cool, dark place for four months.

Decant quickly to remove herbage and minimize exposure to air. Rebottle suitably and label.

Non-potable Alcohols

These include liniments, body rubs, after-shave lotions, skin toners and the like. The alcohols used for these products are for external use only. Again, the restorative properties of the basils and other herbs are conveniently captured in the alcohols.

Isopropyl alcohol, rubbing alcohol and witchhazel are readily available non-potable alcohols.

BASIL BODY RUB

3 large handfuls of basil, any variety
1 handful of wormswood*
(*Artemisia absinthium*)

1 large handful thyme
½ handful rosemary or peppermint
4–6 cups witch hazel

Place all herbs into a wide-mouthed container. Pour in witch hazel to 1 inch of the rim. Seal, shake to expel air bubbles, release those bubbles. Seal and store in a cool dark place for two months.

Decant and discard herbage. Rebottle into conveniently sized container. Use after exercise and make sure your favorite masseur or masseuse has plenty on hand.

*note—not to be taken internally

Non-alcoholic Potables

For a refreshing, soothing change from the common coffees and China teas, brew up some basil instead. A hot holy basil tea recipe is in Chapter 6. You can also make an icy summer cooler that's perfect after hard exercise like building a geodesic dome, running, cycling, swimming or volleyball.

COOL BASIL BREW, STRAIGHT UP OR CUBED

12 sprigs of your favorite basils,
  mix them up
6 sprigs spearmint, orangemint
  or applemint

1 comfrey leaf, medium sized
2 tbs. sweetener—sugar, honey
  or artificial
4–6 cups rapidly boiling water

Method 1:

Twist herbs to slightly crush them and make them more compact. Place inside a teapot or other pot with lid. Pour boiling water over to cover and weight down herbage, if necessary. Steep fifteen minutes.

Strain, discard the herbage, and add sweetener. Cool.

To serve, pour over ice cubes in tall glasses, garnish with a fresh small-leafed basil sprig.

Method 2:

Make as above, but freeze the brew in ice cube trays. When frozen, store the cubes in a plastic bag, *labeled*. Makes 3 trays.

To serve, fill a tall glass with Basil Brew Cubes and add tonic water, seltzer or a dry white wine. Garnish with a fresh sprig of a small leafed basil.

The Perfect Condiment

BASIL PEPPER JELLY

3 cups basil leaves, soft stems
   and flowers, coarse chopped
1 jalapeno, chili or cayenne
   pepper, seeded

4–6 cups of fresh, clear mild
   apple juice
sweetener to taste—sugar, honey
   or artificial

Method 1:

Seed, quarter but do not peel apples. Add just a little water and the apples to a stainless steel, medium-sized saucepan, heat apples slowly until juice flows, and simmer ten minutes. Drain in a jelly bag.

Return apple juice to burner, heat to just below the boiling point and remove from burner. Add basils and hot pepper. Steep for thirty minutes.

Strain, taste to determine if the basil flavor is strong enough. Adjust sweetness. Reheat to a full boil in the stainless steel saucepan. Skim froth from the top and continue to boil for about five minutes.

Pour into sterilized 4- or 8-ounce jelly jars. Garnish with a fresh, very short sprig of basil, making sure it is completely immersed in the jelly.

Seal with ⅛ inch layer of paraffin or seal with conventional canning lid and process in a water bath following manufacturer's directions.

Serve with beef, lamb, mutton, turkey.

Method 2:

Using a packaged pectin:

Brew the basil and hot pepper in the stated amount of liquid, using water instead of juice. Follow package directions, including all of the sugar specified, otherwise your jelly won't jell.

Pastes

Pastes are just that: finely ground, pulverized or chopped herbage sealed with an air-proof agent. Processing the basil immediately releases those volatile essential oils and causes it to oxidize, turning a dark color. Work fast when making any of the pastes and do them in small batches to avoid the not-so-tasty Basil Burn.

Pastes are the essence of herbs—highly concentrated, very convenient to use and store. Use sparingly.

HOW TO MAKE BASIL PASTE IN OIL

5 cups of any variety of basil leaves, soft stems and flowers	1 small, wide-mouthed, tight-sealing 10-oz. jar
about ½ cup of your favorite salad oil	1 tsp. distilled vinegar or basil vinegar

Use your preferred grinding apparatus—mortar and pestle, food processor, blender or very sharp knife and cutting board—to reduce 2 cups of the basil to a coarse chop. Add another 2 cups of basil, reduce to a medium chop. Add the final cup of basil, reduce to a medium chop. Slowly drizzle in oil until all cut leaf surfaces are lightly coated with the oil.

Pack basil paste firmly into jar, filling to within 1½ inches of the rim. Carefully and thoroughly knife out all air bubbles. Float one inch of oil and 1 teaspoon vinegar on top of the paste. (This forms an air-proof seal.)

Label, date and store. Paste can be kept in the refrigerator for about four months. For longer storage, freeze it.

OUT-OF-SEASON PESTO SAUCE

½ cup basil paste
2 cloves garlic, peeled
½ to ¾ cup olive or salad oil
½ to ¾ cup grated Parmesan,
  Sardo, asiago or Romano
  cheeses

pinch of salt
3 tbs. pine nuts, walnut or
  sunflower seeds

In the food processor or blender, grind nuts, add garlic and grind again. Add basil paste. Process very briefly. Add cheese and salt to taste. Process very briefly. With processor running, slowly incorporate oil to your favorite consistency.

Toss on 1 lb. of hot vermicelli, trennette or linguine.

Serves 4–6

HOW TO MAKE BASILLED BUTTER

½ lb. fresh sweet cream butter

1 cup French fine leaf basil,
  destemmed

Method 1:

Melt butter in a 6-inch heavy fry pan. Carefully pour off any clear fluid. Allow to cool.

Quickly stir in basil. Place in covered butter crock and refrigerate. Let stand at least overnight before using.

Method 2:

Soften butter to room temperature. Cream it with a wooden spoon and thoroughly blend in the basil. Form into log and, if desired, roll in additional destemmed basil.

Wrap tightly in plastic wrap or foil and refrigerate.

1. Use on Linda's Basil Beer Bread in Chapter 6.
2. Use to sauté blanched veggies.
3. Stir into pan juices for added flavor.
4. Use on Jan's Basil Buns in Chapter 6.
5. Not suitable for use in butter cream icing.

HOW TO MAKE PASTES PRESERVED IN SOLID WATER

Ice cubes are remarkable for their ability to preserve the quality of basil. When properly stored, they make easy to use, portion controlled, instant additions to soups, stews, stocks and sauces.

1 to 2 cups sweet basil, medium
chop

1 standard-sized ice cube tray
water

Place about 1 to 1½ tablespoons of chopped basil into each ice cube compartment. Slowly add water to not quite fill the tray.

Place in the freezer until frozen. When frozen, remove cubes from tray and store in a plastic bag, expelling air. Don't forget to label and date the bag.

A Fox Hill Farmer's Note:

What to Do with All Those Naked Stems

Even the stems have flavor and the thrifty householder would not dream of discarding them. So what to do?

Get some strong rubber bands and fasten the ends of a number of stems securely. Hang them in the attic to dry. When thoroughly dry, store in brown grocery bags or a cardboard box. (The clothes drier is not an appropriate drying apparatus for naked basil stems. Just ask my dear Donald.)

Throw bundles of dried basil stems on the barbecue to enhance further the flavor of your grilling.

Use the ¼-inch-in-diameter straight stems as skewers.

And, as you snuggle in front of the fireplace, glass of Basil Brandy in hand, casually toss some basil bundles on the fire to perfume the room.

Whole Leaves

HOW TO DRY WHOLE BASIL LEAVES

Drying basil and other herbs is one of the most frequently used methods of preservation. Basil, however, goes through significant flavor changes when it is dried. It is not our preferred method of preserving basil for out-of-season culinary use. When other options are not available, though, dried basil is better than no basil at all!

Supplies:

window screen	basil leaves
cheesecloth or old sheeting	well-ventilated, warm, dark, dry area

Place the basil leaves, one layer deep, on the screen. Cover with cheesecloth or sheeting to protect from dust and light.

Place screen in the well-ventilated, warm, dark, dry area. Check daily and stir occasionally. They should be dry in four to ten days, depending on humidity.

When crisp to the touch, place in an oven set on 100 degrees with the door ajar for about ten minutes to finish drying.

Cool, then immediately store in dark, tight sealing containers. Label, date and store in a cool, dark place. Check the jar daily for three or four days for any signs of moisture or condensation inside the jar. This will cause mold. If moisture is noted, repeat oven-drying process and make sure the leaves are cool to the touch before storing.

Do not store on the top of the refrigerator or the stove or the windowsill. Heat and light can substantially diminish the quality of dried herbs.

HOW TO STORE BASIL BY SALTING

This is an age-old method of preserving basil from days when electricity and refrigeration were not available.

Supplies:

small crock or other non-metallic, wide-mouthed container

kosher, canning or rock salt, but not table salt

basil leaves, your choice of varieties

Place a half-inch layer of salt in the bottom of the clean, dry crock (gallon-sized is easy to handle). Layer in basil leaves, putting a light sprinkling of salt on each layer. Repeat process and press down firmly every ten layers or so, but do not crush.

Fill to within two inches of the top. Press down firmly again. Pour copious quantities of salt on top. Shake and thump on container to fill all air spaces with salt.

Store in a cool, dry place. To use, simply fish out the requisite number of leaves, replacing salt layer as necessary.

HOW TO PRESERVE LEAVES IN OIL

This "Save the Basil" method has the storage advantages of the salting method. It differs only in the preserving medium.

Supplies:

crock or wide-mouthed
  non-metallic container
basil leaves

your favorite salad or olive oil
many, many basil leaves, stems
  reserved
salt

Place a half-inch layer of oil in the bottom of the container. Layer in basil leaves so that each leaf is covered with oil. Sprinkle each layer lightly with salt.

Repeat process, filling to two inches from the top of the crock. Knife along the sides on the crock to release any air bubbles.

If the basil leaves are floating to the top, weight them down with a small plate that just fits inside the crock. Exposure to air can cause mold or discoloration, thus undignifying your ancient preservation efforts.

To use, simply remove the weight and fish out some leaves. Carefully replace weight, maintaining at least a one-inch oil depth above the basil leaves.

HOW TO FREEZE BASIL LEAVES

Many people report good success in freezing basil using both of the following methods. However, we find that it discolors too quickly and looks awful, even though the flavor is retained.

Method 1
Supplies:

shallow pot of boiling water	drying rack
colander	plastic bags and fasteners
large bowl with plenty of ice water	basil leaves

Place a few basil leaves in the colander and quickly blanch in boiling water for no more than one minute. Remove and shock the leaves in ice water. Remove when cool and air dry on a rack. Pack loosely in freezer bags, label, date and freeze.

Method 2
Supplies:

baking sheet	plastic bags and fasteners
basil leaves	

Place basil leaves on the baking sheet one layer deep.
Place in the freezer for one hour until frozen. Pour into plastic bags, seal, label, date and put back in the freezer immediately.

Seeds

Seeds . . . those fragile, dust-sized chalices of life and continuity.

Preserve seeds for two reasons:

1. to sow again in the garden next year, and
2. to use as a seasoning much as poppyseeds, caraway, coriander, dill and sesame seeds are used.

BASIL SEEDS FOR SOWING

Supplies:

large paper bags	storage container
shallow large roasting pan	ripe basil seed florets

Let one basil plant go to flower in your garden. Encourage pollinating insects to fertilize the flowers.

When seed is ripe in late summer to early fall, cut the flowering spikes off of the plant and place in the paper bag without shaking.

You can tell when the basil seed is ripe by bending and shaking a flowering spike a little into the palm of your hand. If tiny black specks float from the spike into your hand, the seed should be sufficiently ripe to germinate.

Tie the top of the bag and hang in a warm, dry, well-ventilated place for a week or so, until the stems of the spike are dry.

Gently rub the florets off the stems through the outside of the bag, leaving all contents inside the bag. In a lightly blowing breeze, slowly pour the contents into the roasting pan. The breeze should blow away most of the floret debris, leaving large floret stems and clean seed in the pan. Pick out the stems.

Pour the seed into a sealable container. Label, date and store in the refrigerator for best germination next season. Baby food jars, pimiento jars, caviar jars and foil envelopes are good storage containers.

BASIL SEEDS FOR EATING

When the flowers on a basil plant are faded for about three weeks, remove them from the plant and place in a bag as described above.

Dry and remove from the chaff as described above.

Now, place your cleaned seeds in a shallow pan and place in a 200-degree oven for about five minutes. Remove pan from oven and allow to cool to room temperature. Store in a small dark jar, labeled and dated.

Flowers

Ah, the subtle sweetness of the delicate, tiny, fragile basil flower . . . in your choice of colors, traditional white or light purple.

Before the florets are fully opened, carefully cut the florets off of the flowering stalk with manicure scissors. Drop immediately into a small container filled with vinegar for future use in salads and soups.

Or for dessert garnishes, candy the florets by dipping in an egg-white wash and dusting with granulated sugar, then air drying until bone dry. Store candied florets in tins, along with your candied violets, rose petals and angelica stems.

If you like to make dried arrangements or plan to make basil potpourri, cut some flowering spikes just as the florets are opening. Fasten six to eight stem ends with a tight rubber band. Hang in a warm, dark, dry, well-ventilated spot for a week to two until very dry. Then store.

10

Basil Beyond the Palate:

Things to Do with Basil When You're Not Eating

Take a Leaf from History . . . or, What They Did with Basil in the Good Old Days

For centuries the ladies of the Mediterranean have been known for their beautiful hair and skin. In the words of Gaylord Hauser, "You are what you eat," and the shine in their hair comes from their diets, rich in cream and oil, enhanced by some routine hair-care treatments.

The following recipe is low-cal because you don't eat it to reap its benefits.

BASIL HOT PACK FOR LOW-CALORIE BEAUTIFUL HAIR

1 cup olive, salad or coconut   1 cup pureed sweet basil
  oil or a combination of oils

Combine ingredients well.

Apply liberally to brushed out dry hair. Massage into scalp and the length of the hair. Cover the hair with a hot, wet towel. Leave on for twenty to sixty minutes.

Shampoo twice to remove oils. Rinse thoroughly.

Apply Basil Glory Rinse and massage into hair and scalp.

BASIL GLORY RINSE FOR BLONDES

½ cup basil leaves   ½ cup of camomile
2 lemons, juiced   1 cup water

Heat water to a boil, add camomile and basil, let steep ten minutes. Strain, add juice of two lemons. Stir.

Use as a final conditioner.

BASIL GLORY RINSE FOR BRUNETTES

½ cup basil vinegar   1 cup water
3 sprigs rosemary

Heat water to a boil, add rosemary and steep ten minutes. Remove rosemary and add basil vinegar. Stir.

Use as a final conditioner.

FOR THE GENTLEMAN'S HAIR

This recipe was given to me by a handsome, debonair Yugoslavian gentleman with a marvelous, wavy head of hair. His baby-blue Cadillac matched his eyes perfectly.

½ cup nettles, fresh or dried
  (caution, handle carefully)
juice of two lemons

3 sprigs rosemary
¼ cup yarrow
2 cups water

Heat water to a boil. Add nettles, rosemary and yarrow. Let steep thirty minutes. Strain, add lemon juice. Use daily.

(You can substitute ¼ cup basil vinegar for the lemon juice.)

SPRING-GREEN SUMMER FACIAL

Spring green is the color, but summer is when this facial feels best, especially after several hours of field work.

1 cucumber, peeled and seeded
1 cup lemon basil, leaves only

2 egg whites, whipped to soft
  peaks

Place cucumber and lemon basil in a blender or food processor. Puree until smooth. Quickly fold in egg whites.

Apply to the face, avoiding the eyes, for five to eight minutes. Lie down, put your feet up, sip a tall glass of Iced Basil Brew.

Wash off the facial with tepid water. Apply skin cream or moisturizer if skin tends to be dry. Go back to work.

EAU DE BASIL

1 pint 75% alcohol (isopropyl)
1½ cups lavender blossoms,
　destemmed

1½ cups any basil variety, chopped
　fine

Combine all three ingredients. Shake well. Store for two to three months, shaking thoroughly every week.

Strain through fine strainer, then restrain through muslin or filter paper to remove herbage. Test strength of fragrance, and if not strong enough, add fresh lavender and basil and again store for two months.

Filter and decant into small bottles. Seal tightly. Use regularly.

BASIL BATH BAGS

This is a fine way to clean out your kitchen cupboards and enjoy a heady, perfumed bath as a reward for your efforts. Check all your dried herbs in your pantry for their potency. If the flavors are not strong, they are no longer culinary quality—but they then become candidates for the bath bags. Caution: do not use peppers in the blends or tumeric (which is a nice yellow dye, as is saffron).

1 cup crushed dried basil
1 cup mixed kitchen herb and
　spice discards
1 orange or 2 lemon peels

18″ × 18″ muslin or large
　handkerchief
rubber band, twist tie, string or
　bottom 12 inches of a nylon
　stocking

Place dried herbs and citrus peel in the middle of the fabric square. Grab edges of fabric to make a pouch. Fasten securely with rubber band, etc. Or . . .

Pour herbs and citrus peel into the foot of a stocking. Knot the open end.

Fasten your Basil Bath Bag to the hot water faucet. Turn on water. Let tub fill slowly and herbs steep. Dive in and soak. Unfasten the Basil Bath Bag from the faucet and use as a gentle skin massager.

Make sure bath bag is securely fastened. It is not one of life's great joys to clean up two cups of wet herbs and peel stuck to the side of the tub, not to mention whatever sticks to your body as you emerge therefrom.

A DUO OF BASIL POTPOURRIS

Potpourri is a carefully balanced mixture of any number of dried herbs, spices, fruit peel, ornamental flowers, fragrant oils and fixatives to hold the delicate fleeting scents.

Just as no two vintages of fine wines or olive oils are alike, so it is with potpourris. Follow the recipe exactly from season to season and you too will find subtle differences in the resulting product's fragrance. And, like most things of lasting value, they take time and patience to make.

These fragrant, herb-laden blends have been created for many, many centuries by countless cultures. They've been used in religious rites, burial rites, to ward off pestilence, as well as for more temporal pleasures—the scenting of a room, a linen closet and the bed. Hedonism is nothing new.

SPICY BASILS WITH SCENTED GERANIUMS, PATCHOULI AND CLEVELANDII SAGE

1 qt. licorice basil leaves	1 cup thyme
1 qt. sweet basil leaves	2 cups patchouli leaves
1 qt. French fine leaf basil leaves	1 cup lemon eucalyptus leaves or
2 cups apple geranium leaves	lemon verbena
2 cups old spice or nutmeg	1 cup Clevelandii sage leaves
geranium leaves	3 oz. vetiver

Again, make sure all plant material is dry.

Carefully mix all dried leaves, tossing gently. Slowly sprinkle on vetiver. Toss again.

Place in an air-tight container and store for a couple of months, stirring occasionally.

SWEET BASILS WITH ROSES, ENGLISH LAVENDER AND ORRIS ROOT

1 quart sweet basil leaves and flowering spikes
2 cups dark opal basil leaves
2 cups dark opal basil flowering spikes
2 cups thyrsiflora flowering spikes
2 cups rose petals
2 cups rose buds

1 cup lavender blossoms
2 cups attar of roses geranium leaves
1 oz. orris root powder
1 oz. sweet flag powder
(For these three, find a drug store that carries botanicals, a craft store or a potpourri supply shop.)

Make sure all plant material is very dry.

Mix all leaves and flowers together, gently. Sprinkle the fixatives—orris root and sweet flag—over all. Toss lightly again.

Place in an airtight container and store for a month or two. Place into small decorative containers.

BASIL AMULET

These pocket assemblages of meaningful content are symbols to many of luck, wisdom, prosperity, wealth and hope. In certain cultures, they have spiritual significance and are sometimes emblazoned with the appropriate religious or spiritual symbols.

1½ cups basil potpourri
mortar and pestle or other crushing device

small fabric or leather pouch
your special good luck token

Place the potpourri in the mortar and pestle. Grind until powdered. Place powder in the pouch along with the good luck charm. Close the pouch opening securely.

BASIL BLISS BAGS

These nifty little pillows are nice in bed. They smell good, and some people feel that they help promote a peaceful night's sleep.

8 cups of your favorite basil   2 12″ × 15″ pieces of percale
  potpourri

Sew three sides of the two pieces of percale together, making a pillowcase.

Add the basil potpourri to the pillowcase. Stitch up the fourth seam, tucking the cut edges inside.

And so, to sleep. May these tales of basil bring you pleasant dreams.

The End
is but the
beginning.
See that tiny speck below
that looks like ink?
If it finds a suitable environment,
it may swell and change . . .
and suddenly there's fresh basil all over again.

.

List of Recipes

Home delivery from Pocket Books

Here's your opportunity to have fabulous bestsellers delivered right to you. Our free catalog is filled to the brim with the newest titles plus the finest in mysteries, science fiction, westerns, cookbooks, romances, biographies, health, psychology, humor—every subject under the sun. Order this today and a world of pleasure will arrive at your door.

 POCKET BOOKS, Department ORD
1230 Avenue of the Americas, New York, N.Y. 10020

Please send me a free Pocket Books catalog for home delivery

NAME _____

ADDRESS _____

CITY _____ STATE/ZIP _____

If you have friends who would like to order books at home, we'll send them a catalog too—

NAME _____

ADDRESS _____

CITY _____ STATE/ZIP _____

NAME _____

ADDRESS _____

CITY _____ STATE/ZIP _____